CATCHING

IRISH
The Summerhaven Novella

KATY
REGNERY

CATCHING IRISH

Katharine Gilliam Regnery, publisher
This book is a work of fiction. Names, characters, places, and
incidents are products of the author's imagination or are used
fictitiously. Any resemblance to actual events, locales, or persons,
living or dead, is entirely coincidental.
All rights reserved, including the right to reproduce this book or
portions thereof in any form whatsoever.
Please visit my website at www.katyregnery.com
First Complete Edition: August 2018
Katy Regnery
Catching Irish: a novella / by Katy Regnery – 1st complete ed.
ISBN: 978-1-944810-35-1

The only way to get rid of a temptation is to yield to it. Resist it, and your soul grows sick with longing.

—Oscar Wilde

For Emma
In memory of Isabel

CHAPTER ONE

Tate Jennings wasn't looking for love.

For romance? Sure.

For a weekend fling? Yes, please.

But love? Blech. No. No, thank you.

Which sort of sucked because love had a goddamned hard-on for Tate.

For as long as she could remember, men had declared their undying devotion for her in that very specific, very dreaded three-word combination. And for as long as Tate could remember, it had made her blood run cold to hear it.

Take for instance, Donald "Duck" Taylor, who in the fifth grade had surprised her at recess with a bouquet of dandelions and his promise to love her "until dead." Tate took that as her cue to play possum. She collapsed to the ground and *pretended* she was dead so Duck's love would find a quick end.

In ninth grade, she recalled a sad episode starring Theodore "Tugboat" Musser, who'd asked her to the homecoming dance by decorating a heart-shaped poster board with the words "I love you, Tate! Will you be mine?" He'd stood on the cafeteria table beside hers, staring down at her, his eyes wide and eager, his smile uncomfortably hopeful.

Just as she was about to mutter, "No, I won't," she

inhaled a bite of chicken nugget and started choking on it. Her friend, Dixie Larue, who was studying to be an EMT, had performed the Heimlich maneuver on Tate with a bit too much enthusiasm, breaking one of her ribs in the process. The half-eaten chicken nugget sailed across the table, landing in a wad on Tugboat's sneaker, and Tate spent the night in the hospital, where the doctor gave her a long list of things she was forbidden to do with a broken rib, including, thank goodness, dancing.

After screwing around with Landon "Bam Bam" Fletcher off and on for most of her junior and senior years at Marathon High School, he'd turned to her one hot, soupy night in the back of his pickup and whispered, "Tate, darlin', I know you don't want to hear it, but I can't hold it inside anymore…I love you."

She'd blinked at him in anger, sat up on the scratchy woolen blanket where they'd just had sex, and reached for her dress. After she pulled it over her head, she looked into the startled eyes of her now *ex*-boyfriend.

"Bam Bam, darlin'," she'd answered, "I know you don't want to hear it, but…we're through." Then she'd slipped on her flip-flops, jumped out of the truck bed, and walked home.

Over the course of the past decade—since Duck, Tugboat, and Bam Bam had rolled the dice and lost—there were countless others who had taken it upon themselves to vomit their affections all over Tate's unwilling heart: one-night stands who wanted more and seemingly solid friendships that crumbled when the guy fell for her. She didn't understand why these men couldn't be content with what she could offer—the "Three *B*s": banging, banter, and bye. But something about her—something that she desperately wished she could identify—made them pursue "more" with her, and it had made her cagey over the years. It had made her angry. It had made her wary. It had made her so damn tired.

But dang it, it hadn't diminished her need for male attention. Her appetite for physical intimacy was as sharp as ever and woefully unmet.

As a charter boat captain in the Florida Keys, Tate had ample opportunity to meet men because she essentially lived in a man's world. In addition to the boatswain, deck hands, mechanics, and steward on her own boat, the other charters in the area were mostly skippered and manned by, well, men. And by and large, her clientele was male—mostly RICH men, looking for a little bit of adventure surrounded by luxury. Tate was well-known for sniffing out the best spots for big-game fishing, and a charter with her wasn't complete until her guests had hauled a kingfish, swordfish, or sailfish onto the marlin deck of her 140-foot QRN yacht and yelled, "Wahoo!"

But crapping where she ate wasn't really Tate's style, which meant that her guests and coworkers were off-limits. Not to mention, Uncle Pete, her guardian and DE FACTO parent since the death of her mom and dad when she was eight, would skin her alive if she played the whore in their own backyard.

So when she was invited to attend the wedding of her old camp friend, Brittany Manion, in New Hampshire, Tate greeted the invitation with anticipation. Not only would she get to revisit the summer camp of her youth where Britt was getting married, but it was the perfect setting for a much-needed fling…if only Tate could find a willing partner.

"Y'all be good up there, now," said Uncle Pete, giving her a hug good-bye after parking curbside at the Marathon airport.

Tate squeezed her uncle tight, closing her eyes and inhaling the comforting mix of EAU DE PETE: bait, fish, and saltwater, rounded out with a hint of mint-flavored chew.

"And YOU take your meds."

"Humph," he muttered close to her ear.

She leaned back, fixing him with a no-nonsense glare. "Uncle Pete, I swear by all that's holy, you're gonna put me in an early grave. You GOTTA take your meds."

His weathered face, complete with a white, salty-dog beard, crinkled into a smile. "Why you so mean to me, Tate Maureen?"

Maureen had been her mother's first name, and Tate was pretty sure her uncle used it just to remind himself of the little sister he'd lost almost twenty years ago.

"I ain't *mean* to you, y'old coot. I CARE 'bout you."

"Aw, you love every hair on my head. Admit it."

Tate chuckled because this man—this grizzly, unlikely character who'd never wanted kids—had taken her in as a broken eight-year-old and done his best to be her father, her mother, her uncle, and her friend. And he'd mostly succeeded, as much as a forty-year-old bachelor could've been expected to. In fact, Pete's voice was the only one on earth that could utter the word *love* without sending an unpleasant shiver down Tate's spine…

"Lord knows I do," she whispered.

…even though she'd never actually responded in kind.

Four-letter curse words? The kind that offended the ladies who sang in the church choir? Tate had no trouble hearing or saying those. But the other one? The *L* word? No. It simply wasn't in her vocabulary, and something instinctual—something innate and involuntary and deeply rooted in her soul—knew that life was much safer if it stayed that way. It was a simple equation: if you didn't offer or accept love, then it couldn't be taken away.

"Promise you'll take the meds, Uncle Pete?" she asked, yanking up the pull handle on her rolling suitcase.

"Yeah, yeah."

"You bein' sassy with me, sir?"

"No, ma'am."

"Alright, then," she said with a curt nod. "And don't forget to pick me up on Sunday at eight fifteen. I'll be waitin' right here."

"Sunday evenin', Tate Maureen," he said with a smile that crinkled his blue eyes. "I'll see you here."

He trudged around the truck to the driver's side, and she watched him drive away until the taillights on his aqua-blue Ford pickup faded from sight.

***

Finian Kelley was missing home.

When he'd left Dublin six weeks ago to work the off-season at the Summerhaven Event and Conference Center in the States, he'd thought it would be good experience that he could parlay into hospitality work when he got home. And it probably *would* be, but being away from Ireland for so long was definitely making him homesick.

Unlike his American-born cousins, Rory, Ian and Tierney, who'd grown up visiting Ireland every other summer, Fin had never traveled beyond the borders of his small emerald island before now. And while he appreciated the easy camaraderie he found with his cousins, he missed his mam, dad, two sisters, and brother. He missed pints pulled from a century-old Guinness tap and the hundred different kinds of rain. He missed a Sunday dinner at mam's and laughing at the muckshites on *You're a Star*. He missed the sad, lovely music coming from the door of every pub on a weekend afternoon and even the sharp-tongued mollies who wouldn't give a proper Guillermo the time of day.

Speaking of women, his last girlfriend, Cynthia, had turned out to be a bleeding weapon with her high ideas about love and forever. Fin had liked her well enough to start—she was small boned with big tits, which was his personal preference—but after a month or two together, she wanted to know where he was all the time: *Who're ya seein' tonight, now? Ya knock the hole off some loosebit later, and I'll hear about it, Fin.* And since one of the lads he went 'round with was her cousin, she'd had his balls in a fucking vise. And what man in his midtwenties wanted that?

Coming to America to work with his cousins on a six-month visa seemed a godsend. He had a good reason to dump clingy Cynthia, and from everything he'd ever heard, American girls were spare arse everywhere. And maybe they were…but not in small New Hampshire towns in November. He'd barely *seen* a single girl his age since arriving, let alone touched one.

Add to this, he'd recently checked out Cynthia's Facebook page and learned that she was *already* seeing someone new: Jamie *fecking* Gallagher, who had a face like a painter's radio and worked at his mam's grocer in a pressed white shirt like every day was Sunday.

Jaysus, he'd thought, staring at the screen in disbelief, *I've been replaced by a bloody knobjockey-looking neddy.*

Seeing Cynthia and Jamie's faces side by side, mugging for the camera, had only made Finian, who hadn't gotten off in weeks, that much more homesick. Which was crazy, because he didn't love her. He'd dumped her. He didn't want to be tied down, right?

Except being "tied down," in every possible sense of the expression, suddenly sounded fecking cla. Because that's what sexual frustration will do, Finian was learning: make a man consider every possible option...just for the chance to throw it in.

And so there was Fin, considering every fecking option and damned grateful that his cousin Rory getting married meant that wedding guests would be coming to stay at Summerhaven for a few days. And maybe—*please, God, maybe*—among those guests there'd be a free and single lass who was horned up by the romance of the weekend...and would let him scratch her itch while she scratched his.

Please.

"Fin," said Rory, leaning over his beautiful bride-to-be, Brittany. "Think you could play something?"

So far, the rehearsal dinner had been a snooze.

Fin was flanked by his cousin's hot, but very taken, fiancée on one side and his stern Aunt Colleen on the other. His eyes had scanned the room for a girl who'd be game for a fling, but so far, he'd come up empty, more's the pity.

At least playing a song or two would liven the place up a bit.

"Ah, sure," said Fin, gesturing to the barn entrance with

a flick of his chin. "M'guitar's over there."

"Get it," said Rory. "I'll make an announcement."

Standing up from his seat, Fin cringed, then froze, as his empty chair crashed to the floor. Beside him, his aunt gasped, her flinty green eyes darting up to capture his.

"Bad luck," she whispered, making the sign of the cross over her chest.

"Ah, come on," he said, ignoring the shiver down his spine as he leaned over to right the chair. "That's just superstition, Aunt Colleen."

"Mí áde," she repeated, this time in Irish.

"Éirigh as." Stop it.

He gave his aunt an annoyed look as he pushed in the chair, but in his heart, Fin knew the truth. Bad luck was coming, whether he liked it or not.

He crossed the room—a barn decorated with white flowers and twinkle lights—to where he'd left his guitar case at the entrance.

"Friends," said Rory, after clanking on his wineglass with a spoon, "you all know that we Havens take our Irish ancestry pretty seriously. As luck would have it, my cousin Finian, who's visiting from Ireland, is staying with us, and he's brought his guitar…"

As Rory droned on about Ireland and Irish music, Fin unbuckled his guitar case and took out his Irish bouzouki.

Imported to Ireland in the 1950s from Greece, the bouzouki had become a staple of Irish pub music over the past sixty-something years. Fin was more than proficient at it, able to play almost any traditional Irish song on his own or pick up a new song after listening for a few minutes.

And as *good* luck would have it, his guitar bore a

shamrock on the back, engraved and stained into the wood. He flipped the instrument over, rubbing the green clover with his fingers. Not quite as good as a rabbit's foot or saint's medal, but the shamrock should still do the trick.

There, he thought. *Bad luck reversed.*

He stood up, looking out over the candlelit room, holding the neck of the guitar, and easing the strap over his head…

And that's when he saw her.

Her platinum-blonde head gleamed in the soft, warm light, catching his eyes and holding them as he tightened his grip on the guitar, physically unable to look away. With his feet planted firmly on the ground, he slid his gaze—*slowly, so slowly*—from the crown of her head to her eyes.

His knees buckled, but he somehow straightened them just before he fell. He felt the jolt in the base of his spine, in the hinge of his jaw, in the tips of his toes. He'd never seen her before, and yet, it was like he *knew* her. Cobalt like the August sky, her eyes sparkled as she stared back him, so brilliant blue in the candlelight, he was hypnotized.

Time stopped, and sound boiled down to a low buzzing in his ears as he stared at her.

Her face was mostly expressionless, her wide blue eyes unblinking as she held his, her shoulders frozen rigid. He knew that Rory was still speaking. He could feel the strings of the bouzouki digging into the pads of his fingertips. But he couldn't move. He didn't know if he'd ever be able to move again.

And then she smiled.

And suddenly his ears tuned into real life again, and his fingers eased off the neck of his guitar. He blinked, taking a deep breath to fill his empty lungs and wondering what had just happened. It was almost as though a spell had been cast, and her smile had released him from—*or into*—the enchantment.

Cailleach phiseogach.

She's a witch. A sorceress.

"Fin? Finian?" He blinked again, looking right, then left, and then focusing on Rory, who was staring back at him expectantly. "Cuz? You, uh, you ready to play?"

"Yeah! Yeah, of course. Comin'," he said, weaving his way through tables, careful not to look back over at the *cailleach*, lest she steal his breath—and his senses—again.

chapter two

Tate hadn't noticed him before he'd stood at the barn entrance staring at her. But now that he was standing beside Rory, playing his guitar and singing some soft Irish lullaby? She couldn't look away. His eyes, downcast in concentration, didn't glance up even once during his singing, which was too bad, since the look he'd given her from the doorway had been hot enough to make Tate twitch between her legs.

She watched his mouth as he sang, imagining it pressed against hers in some dark and anonymous place where they couldn't look into each other's eyes. He sang confidently, occasionally licking his lips in a way that was appealing, if wholly distracting, and she found herself, almost unconsciously, following the words of the chorus he was singing.

"I wish, I wish, I wish in vain,
I wish I had my heart again.
And vainly think I'd not complain."

Tears brightened Tate's eyes and made the room swim as she repeated the words in her head, a glimpse of her parent's faces flashing through her mind. Sepia and warm in her memories, they smiled at her with the kind of undying love she hadn't allowed herself to even dream about since she'd lost them. Like a quick jab to the gut, she felt it—the sharp sting of their loss, all over again—and it made her gasp softly.

I wish I had my heart again.

Closing her eyes and taking a deep breath, she forced herself to change the picture in her mind and think of Uncle Pete, his blue eyes bright against the backdrop of a cerulean sea. Her parents were gone. Pete was alive. Any drop of love left in her dried-up raisin of a heart belonged to him, leaving none for anyone else…including herself.

Mercifully, the soft, heartbreaking song ended, and Tate opened her eyes again as the bawdy chords of a jig filled the air.

"Who is that?" Tate asked her old friend Halcyon Gilbert, who was sitting beside her. The handsome musician's face was alive with joy as he played and sang, and Tate couldn't help wondering if he could be the one she'd been hoping to find this weekend.

"Who? Ian?"

It figures. Of course Hallie only had eyes for her old crush, Ian Haven.

"No, Hal. I know who Ian Haven is. He hasn't changed a bit." This was a not-so-subtle reminder to her friend that Ian was probably still the heartbreaker he'd been as a teenager. "The brown-haired one with the guitar. Some younger Haven brother we never met?"

"Nope. That's their cousin. Finian."

"Ohhhh. *That's* Finian, huh?"

Tate cocked her head to the side. Brittany had briefly mentioned Finian, asking, when Tate called to RSVP to the wedding, if she was bringing a "plus one."

"No. Why? Do I need one?"

"Of course not!" Brittany had laughed. "Want me to set you up?"

"Ha! You haven't changed, little Miss Cupid!"

When they were girls at camp together, Brittany had always been trying to pair up Tate with one of the boys she knew from Boston.

"It's my calling. And Rory has this cousin visiting, Finian, who's single, and I think he would be perf—"

Because she had zero interest in hooking up with one of Brittany's soon-to-be relations, Tate had cut off her friend. "No, thanks."

"Are you sure? He's cute."

He might be cute, but Tate was careful. She wasn't going to get entangled with her friend's husband's cousin. If things went south, it could make things awkward between Tate and Britt.

"I'm sure. Tell me more about the wedding…"

But now, as Finian glanced up at her and grinned? She wasn't so sure she wasn't interested. In fact, there were parts of Tate that felt *very* interested.

His thick brown hair was cut short, and he wore a scruff of beard that defined his jaw and would scratch the inside of her thighs if he kissed her clit.

"He's trouble, huh?"

Hallie shrugged. "I don't really know him."

Hmm. Tate bit her bottom lip, looking away from Finian for a count of ten before catching his eyes again, not *surprised* that they were still trained on her but definitely *gratified.*

It's on.

She just hoped Britt would forgive her if the whole

thing somehow went tits up.

Tate leaned over and kissed Hallie's cheek, suddenly feeling giddy with anticipation. "I gotta powder my nose."

She stood up from her chair, picking it up quickly when it crashed to the ground. After she righted it, she looked back up at Finian, her gaze direct, her invitation universal and unmistakable as she glanced at the barn doorway leading into the dark night and then slid her eyes back to his.

"See you tomorrow, Hal," she said distractedly as she turned and left the table.

She was fairly certain that he wouldn't be playing another song after this one. She'd made it clear what waited for him outside in the darkness. So it annoyed Tate when, after a rousing applause and short pause, the guitar music started up again. Leaning against a tree, several feet away from the barn entrance in the shadow of the candles and twinkle lights, Tate's eyes narrowed as new chords heralded another song and a chorus of Irish voices chimed in to sing.

What? He's playing another song? He's not coming out?

She blinked in shock at the barn, crossing her arms over her chest and deeply affronted that he'd choose to keep playing when she'd been so clear in her offer.

"*Jerk*," she hissed, trying to decide whether she should return to her cabin or go rejoin the dinner.

"Are you callin' me names already?"

She gasped, whipping around to find Finian standing behind her, a wide grin on his handsome face.

"But you're—you're playing the guitar," she mumbled, frowning at him because he obviously wasn't.

"Nah. Me uncle's playin'," he said, chuckling softly at her discomposure.

"Where'd you come from?"

"Back door," he said with a shrug. "Couldn't leave from the same door you did. Might've drawn attention."

"Ah," she said, turning to face him. "So you've done this before?"

"Snogged a lass at a party? Sure. Who hasn't?" He lifted his chin, which made him look cocky. "You had a glad eye for me inside."

"A glad eye?"

"You were lookin' at me like somethin' you wanted to eat."

She wasn't offended. She laughed softly at his arrogant tone. "I wasn't the only one."

"Oh, yeah," he said, his teasing grin lingering. "I mighta noticed you too."

He took a step closer to her, close enough that she could smell him, and his cologne made her gulp softly. Sandalwood. Her favorite.

"I'm Tate," she said, holding out her hand.

"Finian," he answered, taking it.

His palm was rough and warm, dwarfing hers, and though he wasn't as tall as his cousins, he was muscular and lean, and there was an evident strength in his grip.

"I know," she said, stepping closer to him.

His hand slid from hers, landing on her waist, his other hand doing the same. He pulled her firmly against his chest, so that her small breasts—through a thin blouse—pressed against his shirt.

"Your nips is rocks," he noted.

The words made her wet. So simple. So true.

His hands slipped to her ass, pulling her pelvis flush

against his.

"So's your cock."

"Yeah?"

"Yeah."

"You want me to take you against this tree?" he asked, rotating his hips a touch to grind into her.

He was stone hard, long and rigid, and her mouth watered. "Maybe."

"The bark'll scratch your bum, *cailleach*."

She had no idea what the last word meant, but her "bum" was suddenly aching to be scratched. "I'll take my chances."

"So be it," he muttered, his lips dropping to hers in low growl of possession as he lifted her easily, sandwiching her between the tree and his body and groaning as she locked her ankles around his back.

***

Still breathless from exertion, Finian pulled up his pants, zipped the fly, and fastened the button on his pants. *Jaysus, what a ride.*

Flicking a glance up at her, he watched Tate smooth her skirt and slip her feet back into her shoes.

Her face was serene in the moonlight, her platinum head almost glowing in the soft light. For no good reason he could fathom, it made him feel a sudden tenderness for her.

"You all good?" he asked.

She nodded. "Sure."

He had no reason not to believe her, and having dispensed with gentility, his mind moved swiftly on to the next order of business: his ego. "So…was it, um, okay?"

She reached behind and rubbed her backside through

her dress, offering him a cryptic smile. "Scratched bum, as promised."

It wasn't the declaration he was looking for, but asking again would seem desperate. Besides, he knew the truth: he'd come too quickly.

But hell! It had all happened so damn fast. They shook hands. Suddenly, he had her pressed against the tree and they were kissing. Her fingers grappled for his buckle. He shoved her panties aside. Bam! He was in. He'd thrusted four or five times and then—Wait! Fuck!

"Shit! We didn't use a—"

"I'm on the pill," she said. She cocked her head to the side and narrowed her eyes. "Are you the type of asshole who would fuck a girl if he wasn't clean?"

"No."

"Then we're all good," she said, leaning back against the tree with a sigh.

It was dark, but the ambient light from the barn shone on her face, and if he wasn't mistaken, there was a tiny, almost invisible, tick in her jaw.

"Sure you're okay?" he asked.

"Right as rain," she said. She glanced up at the path, which was lit by tiki torches to show the way back to the cabins. "I think I'll go to bed."

Something in him flared—something like chivalry but slightly less noble, making him wonder: Did he fear for her safety? Or was he hoping for seconds?

"I'll walk with you."

She smiled at him, but it wasn't a real smile, not like the one she'd given him inside the barn. Her eyes didn't sparkle. "No, thanks. Not necessary."

"Hey, now! I'm being a gentleman. I'm *offering*."

"You're no gentleman," she said, pushing away from the tree. "And I'm *declining*."

"So that's it?"

"Did you want me to write you a poem?" she asked, a slight edge in her voice. "I'm all out of stickers."

He stared at her. "Seems like…I don't know…a bit cold."

She chuckled at him, but it wasn't a warm, confident sound. It was tinny. Hollow. Like the smile she'd just given him. "I'm okay with that. 'Night, Fin."

He watched her go—the way her dark skirt, which had been hitched around her hips only moments before, now brushed the back of her thighs as she walked away, up the path and out of sight.

And damn it all if he didn't feel a little used, a little bruised, and a lot wondering if his performance was so underwhelming that she didn't even accept his offer to escort her home. Was it that bad? Christ, it had felt great to him no matter how fast it had happened. And hadn't she bitten his ear? What was that all about? Hmm. Fin pulled at his ear lobe with his thumb and forefinger. It had been months since he'd been with someone, but he'd never had complaints before. Maybe his fat dick wasn't enough if he came in under five minutes. *Shite*. Maybe she was going to tell Brittany how much it had sucked, and Brittany would tell Rory, and Rory would tell Ian, and—*Jaysus, Mary and Joseph!*—it'd be all over Limerick by the time it got back to him.

He could hear it now: his brother and sisters heckling him about it until the end of time. *Remember the lass from New*

Hampshire? From Rory's wedding? Should have named you Johnny-come-quickly!

Shite, shite, shite.

He needed to prove to her that he could do better.

Next time, he'd go slowly.

Next time, he'd show her that he was capable of bringing a woman to the very brink of heaven before opening the pearly gates and shoving her inside. He'd make her see fireworks. He'd make her see goddamned bloody stars.

"Next time," he muttered, turning back to the barn and grumpily wondering if "next time" was even in the cards.

chapter three

"How was *that*?" asked Fin, panting in Tate's ear.

They'd seen each other at the wedding, of course, her eyes unable to stop seeking his throughout the ceremony and his having the same problem. As Rory and Britt made their way back down the aisle as man and wife, Fin had grabbed her hand, pulled her through a side door, down a flight of stairs, and into the basement of the church.

Tearing at one another's clothes, their teeth clashing as they kissed, he'd spun her around in front of a long table covered with choir music, leaning over her, his front to her back.

"You want it?" he'd demanded roughly, his breath hot against the back of her neck. "Say it."

"Yes!" she'd cried, soaked with anticipation after forty-five minutes of hot glances in the sanctuary upstairs. "I want it!"

"How much?"

"Now!" she'd yelled, her voice breaking with frustration.

He'd hiked up her dress, yanked down his pants, lined himself up, and thrust into her, his teeth biting into her shoulder as she gasped. He was huge and throbbing, hard as a rock but smooth as velvet, massaging the walls of her sex with every successive pump of his hips. Reaching around, he'd put two fingers in her mouth, and she'd sucked them greedily. When he'd reached for her breasts and tweaked her nipples through the bodice of her dress, she'd bitten down on one so hard that he'd growled in pain, then slammed deeply into her body just like she wanted him to.

And fuck, it was fast and furious and...*delightful*.

All of it. Right up until the very end, when he took his fingers, slick from her mouth, and rubbed them in raspy circles against her throbbing clit. She'd screamed then, unable to hold back the maelstrom inside.

He'd come violently into her, groaning like a dying man, the hot spurts of his cum satisfying to both of them on a base and visceral level.

Now she only had two gripes.

One, it was over too soon—the latent waves of bliss, of wildly contracting muscles, perfect yet maddening as they slowed.

And two, as her heart rate returned to normal, she felt so terribly, indescribably lonely that she closed her eyes against an unexpected rush of tears and forced her mind to go blank.

His voice, asking about his performance, made her refocus her attention.

How was that?

He leaned over her back, the buttons of his shirt digging through the thin material of her dress, his cock still deeply embedded within her. "Tate. Was it okay?"

Was it "okay"? No, Fin. It was excellent. It was first-rate, grade-A fucking.

"Let me up," she said softly.

He backed away from her, and she felt his hot flesh slip from her body. Her palms were flat on the table, and she used them to push herself upright on shaky legs, pulling down and smoothing her dress with her back to him.

She looked up, and before her, on the wall, was a poster of a rainbow. Under it, it read, "God is Love. God is Real. Love is Real."

Tate clenched her jaw.

"Hey," said Finian from behind her, tapping her on the shoulder. "Are you okay?"

She spun to face him. "Fine."

"Sure?"

She nodded, uncertain if she trusted her voice not to waver.

"You're beautiful," he said, reaching for her flushed cheek.

Tate sidestepped his touch. "You don't need to say that."

"Why not? It's true."

Whatever. She grabbed her purse off the table.

"I hope…" he started.

She could see what he wanted. She knew that he needed some sort of reassurance that she'd enjoyed herself, that he'd performed well. But the sign on the wall made her batten down the hatches, made her feel frightened and mean.

Her tone was terse. "You hope *what?*"

"I hope that was good for you," he said simply, his hands loose by his sides.

It occurred to her to ask him if he'd ever fucked a woman before. Didn't he feel the bites on his fingers? The way she'd come apart when he'd fondled her clit? The way her body had shaken uncontrollably, her innermost muscles clenching around him like an obscenely tight glove? The sounds of her moans and cries? The scream when she'd orgasmed? Had he missed all of that? Was it necessary to rehash it?

She wasn't in the mood to stroke his ego. If he'd somehow missed the fact that she'd orgasmed big, that wasn't her problem. She took a deep breath and sighed. "Reception starts soon. We better go."

He'd been smiling hopefully at her, but now he frowned. "You're hard to please."

Oh, Lord. "I didn't say I was unhappy."

"Didn't say you were happy either." He took a deep breath and let it go loudly in consternation. "Why'd you say yes in the first place?"

"Because I wanted you to fuck me."

He blinked at her. "Jaysus, but you're stone cold."

That was, in fact, what she was trying to project, but it really bothered her to hear him say it. It stung for reasons she couldn't begin to understand and had no interest in unpacking. She crossed her arms over her chest. "Isn't that what every guy wants?"

"Is it?" His brows knitted together as he looked at her. "I don't know."

She laughed at him. "It is. I promise."

"Me last girlfriend," he said, reaching down to fasten his tuxedo pants, "was clingy as shit. Demanded to know where I was goin', and when, and with whom. Constantly ridin' my ass, you know? I thought I hated it. But now..."

"Now what?"

His eyes were sad as he stared back at her. "I don't

know."

"You don't seem to know very much," she muttered, heading for the door, careful not to look up at the poster that proclaimed, "Love is Real," which—in her opinion—was irresponsible as fuck. Sure, it *might* be real, but it could die, and when it did, it flattened a person. Tate knew the anguish of that loss, and she never wanted to experience it again.

"Hey, hey, hey," he said, his footsteps quick as he caught up with her on the stairs. "Wait up."

"Why?"

"I…Jaysus, I don't get you."

"What don't you get?"

"It's like you don't even want to chat. You only want…"

"What?" she asked, looking at him over her shoulder. "Sex? What's wrong with that? I can't have needs like you? I can't feed the need without getting—what was it, again?—'clingy as shit'?"

She continued up the stairs, grateful to find a mirror at the top. Wearing her hair in a bob had some definite pluses, like the fact that she could run her hands through the thin, silvery-gold strands and voilà! Her coif was like new.

Behind her, Fin's face appeared, and she looked their reflections for a moment: at the tempting pout of his lips, at the mixture of satiety, warmth, and confusion in his green eyes. It was his eyes that had first captivated her last night in the candlelit barn—the way they'd held hers with such earnestness, like he'd never seen anything as remotely wondrous as Tate. It had coaxed real emotion from her, and she'd given him a rare and genuine smile in thanks for the compliment of his admiration.

"You ever been in love?" he asked her reflection.

Her nostrils flared. "Don't believe in it."

"What?" he asked, his lips tilting up like she was kidding. "How can you not *believe* in it?"

"Because it doesn't exist," she said, running her hand through her hair again before sidestepping away from the mirror. "Love is a myth."

"Jaysus, you're cagey."

"I'm…cagey?" she asked him, looking around for a door that wouldn't force her to parade past the wedding party, who were greeting guests at the front of the church. She spied a double door down the corridor that appeared to lead directly out to the parking lot. *Bingo.*

"Never met a girl who didn't believe in love," said Fin, following at her heels.

"Now you have," she said, pushing open the doors and stepping outside.

"Why is that?" he asked. "Why don't you believe in it?"

Tate huffed in annoyance. "What's with the third degree?"

"We've fucked twice. I feel like we should get to know each other."

"Ha! What for?"

He chortled behind her, and she turned to face him, raising her eyebrows like she expected an answer.

"You're somethin'," he said.

"Everyone's something."

"Somethin' different," he clarified. His lips twitched, and he offered her a teasing smile. "Give me a ride back to camp?"

"What kind?"

"Car'll do."

"Why are you smiling?"

"Can't I smile?" he asked. "Or do you not believe in smiles either?"

She lowered her chin and put her hands on her hips. "You can smile. And you can have a ride back, but let's just be super clear about one thing, okay? We're having a fling this weekend, Finian. It's fucking. We're not friends. We're not anything."

He stared at her, as though processing her words.

"To be clear, we may fuck again, or we might not. Either way, it doesn't mean anything. Don't read into it. Don't get attached," she said, leveling him with her eyes. "Understand?"

He took a deep breath, his jaw clenched, his eyebrows still furrowed, his index finger sliding slowly across his lips in thought.

"I have a question," he said.

"For God's sake! What?"

"Can we go back to the part about fuckin' again?"

Suddenly—without any warning and for the second time since she'd met him—she felt *real emotion* course through her veins, warming her body, catching her off-guard. Surprise. Amusement. Happiness. And she did something she rarely did with a man she was fucking: she laughed. Or more accurately, she snorted. The sound chortled through her nose, thoroughly surprising her and leading to a gale of unexpected giggles.

When she looked up at him, she saw he was laughing too. Not as hard as her. Not as much. But the smile on his face reached his eyes…and made them sparkle.

"We'll discuss it in the car," she said, leading the way.

***

Halfway back to the camp, Tate had reached for Fin's cock and started stroking it through his pants. When he'd been about to come, he'd pushed her hands away and demanded that she pull over. As soon as she'd cut the engine, he'd released the beast, dragged her onto his lap, and speared her quickly.

Rocking against him, she'd taken his load again, mewling against his neck as she came, and this time Fin hadn't needed to ask. She'd come. He'd felt the gathering, the quivering, and the tight clench of her pussy around his cock before she cried out. Only then had he given himself over to his own orgasm, holding her tightly and whispering filthy things in her ear.

When they'd arrived at Summerhaven, she'd parked at the far side of the camp parking lot, and they'd kissed and groped for a while before she had preceded him to the reception. He'd arrived soon after, straightening his shirt and running a hand through his hair.

He couldn't get enough of her.

He knew she was leaving tomorrow.

He knew she lived in Florida.

He knew he would likely never see her again.

But for the first time in his life, Finian was learning that there was a delicious sort of intensity in a love affair when your time was finite. The distance that would imminently separate them made every second precious, heightened the fleeting sense of every touch, and made every word powerful. In the strangest way, this girl who disavowed love and wanted so badly to belong to no one belonged to *him* for this millisecond in time, and he welcomed that sense of possession because it was only temporary. For now, and *only for now*, she was his, and he wanted to soak up every second with her.

Seated at the same table, they sat side by side, fondling each other under the table near constantly and tacitly daring one another not to react openly or draw attention to what they were doing. It was a torturous but delectable game, a shared and dirty secret that kept him semierect throughout toasts and dinner.

Twice they'd danced, though both times he'd needed to head outside afterward to cool down. She smelled like him. She smelled like his cum and some perfume that she was wearing, and fuck if it didn't make it impossible not to want her again, though he'd already had her thrice in twenty-four hours.

As the reception wound down, she visited across the room with her friend Hallie, and Finian found himself staring at her like a lovesick teenager, wondering if she'd invite him to stay overnight with her and desperately hoping that she would. Whereas he shared lodgings with his cousin Ian, Tate had her own cabin with a big, queen-sized bed. For all that they'd fucked, they hadn't been naked with each other, and it was all Finian could think about—their bodies entwined, skin to skin, until dawn rent the skies.

The sweet torment of will-she or won't-she kept him on his toes, his cock leaping with hope when she paused in her conversation with Hallie to look over at him. But he had a distinct feeling that if he pushed her, she'd push him away. He didn't know if he bought her whole "love is a myth" routine, but he was certain that *she* believed it. He also had a feeling that her theories on love were more about self-preservation than grounded conviction, but it didn't matter. He wasn't playing a long game here, so he needed to step lightly. If he pressured her, she'd tell him to go fuck himself, and that'd be the end of the hottest and most spontaneous weekend of sex he'd ever had.

So what's the killer move? he wondered, watching her smile at her friend.

Space.

Distance.

Feigned indifference.

If he acted like he didn't care whether they fucked or not, he had a feeling that she'd be ten times more likely to invite him over.

"Well, that's me," said Finian to his Uncle Ted, who sat beside him at the table. "I'm knackered."

"Headed to bed, Finian?"

"Yeah. Think so," he said. "Are ya drivin' back to Dartmouth tonight?"

"Colleen sleeps best at home," said his uncle. "I guess we'll see you at Christmas?"

Finian nodded, though he felt a sharp twinge in his heart. Being away from his family at Christmastime this year was going to be hard. "I guess so."

"You know," said his uncle, "you should see Boston before you head home. It's a great city."

"Oh, yeah?"

"Sure. Visit the Druid. Colleen says it's the best Guinness in America."

And since—aside from fucking Tate again—a pint of

Guinness was presently at the top of Fin's longings, he nodded. "You know? I think I'll do just that. Ian said it's quiet here next week. Maybe I'll take a few days off."

"You should!" said Uncle Ted. "Make the most of your visit. Before you know it, you'll be home, son."

The pain in his heart eased at this suggestion, and he felt gratitude toward his uncle.

After kissing his aunt on the cheek and wishing her a safe trip home, Finian made his way across the room, careful to lock eyes with Tate as he passed her but also quick to look away. If she wanted to see him later tonight, it was up to her to suggest it, though he'd be lying if he didn't confess that he was hoping—with every fiber in his body—for an invitation.

chapter four

"Fin! Wait up!"

Tate had seen him leave, wondering why—after staring at her across the room for the past hour—he didn't even stop by to say good-bye. Not that it hurt her feelings. Not that she cared. She didn't. No attachments, right? Right. But was she wrong to expect civility?

A few yards up ahead of her on the path, he stopped walking and pivoted to face her, but he didn't move or say anything. Fast-walking in heels, she was out of breath by the time she caught up with him.

"Hey," she said, stopping before him, her chest heaving from the exertion. His eyes flicked down for an ogle, then trailed back up to her face.

"Hey."

"Are you…leaving?"

"Thought I would." He shrugged. "Long day."

"You're going to bed?" she asked, blurting out the words.

No, they hadn't made a plan to get together after the reception, but after all of the under-the-table teasing, she'd assumed that they would be.

Fin reached up and scratched his cheek. "My uncle said

I should check out Boston. I was thinkin' about headin' over there tomorrow. Thought I'd get online and…you know, make a plan, see what's what."

"I'm going to Boston tomorrow," she said, vaguely aware that they'd started walking in the direction of her cottage.

"Flyin' home?" he asked.

"Yeah. Evening flight. Two o'clock check-in." She put her hand on his shoulder to brace herself, then lifted her feet, first one, then the other, and took off her shoes, holding them on her fingers by the sling-back strip of leather. "Ohhhh. That's better."

He'd stopped walking when she touched his shoulder, but now he looked at her, a slight smile on his lips. "You good?"

"You ask me that a lot," she said.

"Mmm," he hummed noncommittally.

What was up with him? He seemed…different, somehow. Not as eager. Not as needy. Maybe he'd finally caught on to the fact that he'd made her come in the car and didn't feel the need to prove himself anymore? Then again, it occurred to her, if that was the case, and he was finished with their short and filthy arrangement, he could have just said good-night and good-bye at the top of the path. Instead, he was walking her home.

What were they talking about? Oh, right. Boston.

"So you're going to Boston tomorrow?" she asked.

"Thinkin' about it," he said, shoving his hands in his pockets.

"Need a ride?" she blurted out.

He stopped walking.

Tate felt her cheeks flush, and she flinched, walking past him slowly and wondering where in the Sam Hill had *that* offer come from? It was almost like she wanted to spend more time with him…but why? What was the point? He lived here—not even here, in *Ireland*—and she lived in Florida! What the fuck was the point of getting to know him better? Not that she wanted to get to know him better. Did she?

Fuck. Did she?

Warning bells were going off in her head because getting to know someone better could lead to feelings, and feelings could lead to an attachment, and an attachment could lead to lo—

No. No, no, no. Back up. No getting to know him better. No feelings. And definitely no attachments. *Take it back. Take it back before he answers!*

She whipped around to face him, expecting his face to be eager, which would make retracting her offer so much easier.

But he didn't look eager at all. In fact, if he looked like anything, it was sort of casually thoughtful.

"You know? That'd be grand as long as you're headed that way anyway. You'd be savin' me bus fare."

And—yet *again*—it happened.

Like a colt with the right trainer, who somehow knew how to ease its behavior from skittish to calm, Fin had just managed to do that for Tate. And because no one had ever handled her so easily before, it disarmed her. It made her comfortable. She started walking again and kept the offer on the table.

"Want gas money?" he asked, stepping into place

33

beside her.

"No. I want you to come to my cabin and fuck me again, and we'll call it even. Deal?"

He chuckled softly but didn't reach for her hand or put his arm around her shoulders or otherwise get sentimental and clingy.

"Yeah," he said as they continued down the path. "Deal."

***

Finian had gotten his wish.

They were naked in her bed.

But in a strange twist of events, she was the first girl ever who, postsex, didn't try to cuddle into his side, lying on his arm until he lost feeling in it and making him sweat from their combined body heat. No. This girl flipped onto her back beside him, yawned several times, then closed her eyes and fell asleep. No reassurance needed. No tentative hopes that they'd stay in touch after tomorrow. No tears that their "magical weekend" was coming to an end.

Nothing.

Maybe she really *didn't* believe in love, which was so odd, it was almost freakish. But he'd never met a girl less emotionally needy or more guarded.

And yeah, okay, he *kind* of liked it. It was so weird and unusual, this level of casual. Some girls *claimed* to be this casual, but they were almost always lying.

But on the other hand, for the first time that he could ever remember, he sort of *wanted* a little more. He sort of wanted to pull her back against his chest, wrap an arm around her waist, and fall asleep beside her.

Madness, Fin. Utter lunacy.

That's just wantin' what you can't have, boyo.

He rolled to his side, watching her sleep, tracing the lines of her face with his eyes. She was quite lovely, her features delicate and the column of her neck graceful. But it was hard—*really* hard—to get to know her. And while part of him was intrigued by the challenge, more of him could see that she was a wounded thing, like a bird with a broken wing or a cat with a thorn embedded deeply in its paw. Wounded animals, even if they desperately needed help and care, didn't know how to seek it and often didn't recognize it when offered. Instead, they were prone to biting, to fighting, to running away and finding a quiet place to die.

He sighed, rolling onto his back and staring at the shadows on the ceiling as a quiet melancholy filled him. There was no catching this girl, he decided, as his heavy eyes slowly closed. There was no *having* her, so his only option was to simply *enjoy* her until they said good-bye.

***

The next morning, Tate woke up alone, which should have been a good thing but strangely wasn't.

She'd been too tired to kick Fin out last night and ended up falling asleep beside him after two rounds of epic sex. But twice during the night when she woke up—once to pee and once because some late-night revelers had walked past her cabin at dawn—she'd been oddly comforted by his presence. Oddly, because she couldn't actually remember the last time she'd slept beside someone. It simply wasn't something she did very often.

The second time she woke, as the grayish light of early dawn flooded through the window, she'd rolled to her side and watched him sleep for a while; his face in repose was beautiful, his lips slightly parted, his long eyelashes thick and dark, his bare chest rising and falling in peaceful sleep. She'd watched him until her heart ached for no reason she could name, until her eyes had felt heavy, and she'd closed them only because she couldn't keep them open anymore.

And now he was gone.

Sliding her hand from under her pillow with a sigh, she rested it on the pillow he'd used last night, settling her fingers in the indent made by his head. The cotton was cool, so he'd likely been gone for a while. *Oh, well. At least you still have today*, she thought, a bit of melancholy making her sigh again.

Wait. What? She yanked back her hand like the fabric was on fire, staring at the pillow with dismay.

At least you still have today?

"Fuck, Tate," she hissed, swinging her legs over the side of the bed to sit up and purposely putting her back to Fin's side.

Out the window, she could see wedding guests, casually dressed in jeans and sweaters, heading up the path to attend Rory and Brittany's wedding breakfast, and she tried to breathe easily, though her pounding heart made it difficult.

"You got attached. You fucking got attached," she whispered, her tone gritty with self-disgust. "*Not* acceptable."

She showered and dressed quickly, self-preservation making her haul ass, eager to find Fin and tell him that she wasn't able to give him a ride to Boston after all. They needed a clean break. Today. As soon as possible.

Hurrying up the path, dressed in jeans, a black blouse, and a black leather jacket, she encountered him sitting on a wooden porch swing near the dining hall, browsing on his phone.

He looked up at her.

"Hi," he said simply.

"Good morning," she answered formally.

"Sleep well?"

"Hmm," she hummed, her stomach in knots.

"Hmm," he repeated, narrowing his eyes and cocking his head to the side. His glance flicked to the hands by her sides, which she kept balling and releasing. His voice was cool and measured when he spoke. "I'm pretty sure you're about to tell me why I can't have a ride to Boston today."

She shoved her hands in her jacket pockets and nodded. "I think it's best."

"Because…why? Hmm. Let's see…" He tapped his lips. "Because last night sucked?" He stared so deeply into her eyes, she couldn't look away. "No. That's not it. We both enjoyed last night."

"I just think—"

"What? That I might try to make this into somethin' more? Borrow a car, drive to Florida, profess my undyin' love and declare I can't live without you?"

It *did* sound ridiculous when he put it like that.

"You told me not to get attached," he said, standing up and facing her. "I listened."

But I, apparently, didn't.

"Listen, Tate," he said, his voice relaxed. "I assume you have to drop off your car at the airport in Boston this afternoon, right?"

She nodded.

"So give me a ride, I'll take you out to lunch at the Druid to thank you, and we can say good-bye there."

"The…Druid?"

"They pull the best Guinness pints in Boston and have Irish stew on the menu." His lips tilted up in the slightest smile as he started walking toward the dining hall doors. "You wouldn't deprive me of some real Irish stew, would you, now? Not when I'm so far from home? Missin' my mam and da…and me wee sister Bess?"

Was it her imagination, or was his accent suddenly twice as strong as it had been two minutes before? She fell into step beside him, letting him open the door for her and preceding him into the bustling breakfast room.

"Do you really have a sister called Bess?"

"Nah," he said. "We don't call her that anymore. It's Elizabeth now, thank you very much."

"Is she your only sibling?"

He shook his head, grabbing a plate at the fruit salad bar and handing it to her before taking one for himself. "I'm one of four."

"Any brothers? Or just sisters?"

"I have one brother and two sisters. Callum, Elizabeth, Grace, and me."

"The baby," she said, rolling her eyes as she scooped from fresh pineapple onto her plate. "Why am I not surprised?"

"I don't know," he said, reaching around her for a spoonful of strawberries, his forearm brushing her waist in the process. "Why are you not surprised?"

She turned to look at him.

Wait. How had this happened?

She was going to tell him he *couldn't* have a ride to Boston, and somehow she'd agreed not only to give him a ride but to have lunch with him too and was presently choosing breakfast fruit like she hadn't had a full-blown panic attack fifteen minutes ago. How did he keep doing this? How did he know exactly how to put her at ease without coming on too strong? Or too pushy? Or too needy?

"The youngest in the family is often the most underrated, y'know."

She looked up at him. "How's that?"

He grinned. "Because they weren't plannin' on you. They never saw you comin'."

***

The Druid turned out to be exactly the sort of spot that Fin had been longing for, but there was no way around it: lunch was spoiled before it even began.

Halfway through their meal—fish and chips for Tate and Irish stew for him—a sense of longing, even stronger than that for home, had taken over his mood, and he found himself less gregarious and more peevish as the minutes ticked down. It all boiled down to one thing: he didn't want to say good-bye to Tate.

His life in New Hampshire had been lonely before she showed up; he wasn't in any rush to get back to it.

Fuck me, he thought, staring at her pretty face across the table and remembering, vividly, what it looked like when she was in the throes of orgasm, *I really don't want to feckin' say good-bye.*

And yet, by his calculations, he had about ten minutes left before she finished her last sip of beer, stood up, and walked out, heading for the airport.

"So you're off to Florida," he said.

She nodded. "You ever been?"

"Never been anywhere but home and New Hampshire," he said. "Well, and now here."

"It's warm there," she said. "And the water's turquoise."

"What do you do there?" he asked, realizing he knew very little about her and suddenly desperate to make the most of their dwindling minutes.

"I run fishing charters for rich assholes."

And fuck me again, but she screws like a champion, looks like a goddess, and she's a skipper and fisherman? Fin's heart couldn't take much more.

He hid his expression of undiluted yearning by sipping his beer as she asked, "What about you?"

"Here? Maintenance on my cousins' camp."

"And at home?"

Would she think less of him for not having been to university? "Mechanic."

"Cars?"

He nodded, looking up at the waiter and gesturing for another Guinness. Once she left, he was going to get good and langered to ease whatever ache remained.

"Ever worked on a DeLorean?" she asked.

His jaw dropped open.

There was only one reason she'd ask that specific question. And fuck, but the chances of any American girl knowing the manufacturer of the most iconic car ever produced in Ireland was so inconceivable, it made this lass a unicorn and no mistake.

Suddenly, he couldn't fucking bear it.

"Don't go," he murmured, leaning across the table. "Not yet."

Her eyes clouded with disappointment as she leaned back in her seat. "Come on, Fin. Don't do this."

Fuck. Shite. And balls. He'd been so cool with her, and now he'd gone and mucked it all up. It made him angry. With himself. With her. With the whole situation of meeting a deadly fierce American girl who fucked for fun and made him laugh and knew that DeLoreans used to be made in Ireland. And he couldn't have her. He had to let her go.

"I guess so," he bit out.

"I *told* you—"

"I know what you bloody told me," he snapped, lifting the new pint of Guinness to his lips and downing a full quarter before coming up for air.

She gulped softly, staring back at him, her expression conflicted. Finally, she whispered, like it was a secret she had no business sharing, "I had fun."

"Well, thank the dear Lord for that," he muttered, feeling mean.

Leaning to her right, she grabbed the straps of her purse and lifted them onto her shoulder, still facing him.

"Kiss me good-bye?" she asked, standing up and staring down at him.

He looked up at her, hating her. Hating himself more.

Then he stood up and clasped her face in his hands, his lips falling fast and angrily onto hers. He kissed her hard, right smack in the middle of the pub, ignoring the catcalls around them that grew louder as the kiss softened and turned tender. He pulled her into his arms, sliding his tongue against hers again and again, his fingers curling into fists on her lower back as he tried to let her know—the only way he could—how much he wished they had more time.

But they didn't.

When the kiss ended, she opened her eyes, and damn if they weren't glistening. They *were*. Fin would stake his life on it, and it made him stupid. He rested his forehead on hers. "Stay."

"I can't," she whispered, backing out of his arms. "Fin...don't call me, don't—"

"Don't feckin' worry," he bit out.

"Sorry," she murmured. "Good-bye."

He watched her go, his heart hurting like hell.

"Mate," said a guy at the adjacent table, his eyes sympathetic. "I think you're fucked."

Fin sat down and chugged his beer before turning to the bloke. "I think you're right."

chapter five

Four Months Later

"Captain Tate," said the white-haired gentleman, "on behalf of the New Greenwich Men's Association, we want to thank you for leading such an exciting and successful charter!"

As his five friends clapped in agreement, Mr. Franklin handed over a thick envelope to Tate that contained the tips for herself and her crew. And from the feel of it, the NGMA charter had been a success.

"Thank you, Mr. Franklin," she said with a grin. "And don't you forget to send me a picture of that sailfish on the wall of your den, you hear?"

"I will do, Tate! I promise. She's a beauty."

"Sure is."

She exchanged hugs and handshakes with the six gentlemen before waving good-bye from the dock. When her guests were out of sight, she looked over her shoulder at her boatswain, Tom. "Get her in shipshape? I'll divvy up what's here."

"Aye, aye, Cap," said Tom, turning to his crew of four deckhands and calling out a list of tasks from spraying down the decks to securing the tender.

Her lead steward, Jones, came up from below decks

with four snow-white, recently laundered and folded towels in his arms. "Good job this charter, Jones."

"Thanks, Cap."

She held up the envelope. "Good tip too."

Jones smiled and nodded. "Glad to hear it, ma'am."

Tate glanced at the towels. "Restocking the hot tub area?"

"Aye, Cap."

"Carry on."

There were some charter captains, of course, who didn't exercise such formality with their crew, but Tate had learned the old ways from Uncle Pete, and they'd served her well. It didn't matter the age or experience of her crew; they respected her as their captain because she insisted on it. There was never any confusion about who was in charge, and they'd be fired the second they showed Tate the slightest measure of disrespect or insubordination.

In return, Tate made smart choices, offered high-end service, and after taking a 20 percent cut of tips, split the rest evenly among the crew. For the five-day cruise they'd just completed? Each of her eight crew members would probably make a gratuity of more than one thousand dollars each. It was no wonder her employee retention rate was so high.

"Skip," said her mechanic, Julio, who fell into step beside her as Tate headed for the bridge, "you got a minute for bad news?"

"Do I have a choice?" she asked.

"Nope," said Julio, scratching the back of his perpetually sunburned neck. "I hate to say it, but we got some hull osmosis going on. Doesn't look good."

Hull osmosis? Fuck. That meant blisters on the bottom

of the boat.

Tate sighed, putting her hands on her hips and her sunglasses on her head.

"It's only four years old."

Julio nodded. "Which means it's a manufacturer defect."

"It's got to be covered in the warranty."

"It *is*, Skip," said Julio. "It is, and that's the good news."

"So what's the bad?"

"Warranty stipulates you gotta report it when you find it so they can fix it right away."

"It's just osmosis. It's not like it's going to sink my ship," said Tate, feeling annoyed. February and March were moneymakers for her, and she knew—as well as any captain—that the cure for osmosis took time. A boat needed to be hauled out and dry-docked, then sanded down so that the fiberglass could be repaired. It was time-consuming as fuck and would have her boat on land for the next six to eight weeks.

"It's a busy season!" she exclaimed.

"Skip? It's Florida. It's *always* a busy season," he said, giving her a rueful look. "Do you have cancelation insurance?"

She shook her head. "Nope."

"You got friends who can take your charters? Your uncle?"

"Maybe."

"If I may speak freely, ma'am?"

"Go for it."

"It's a nine-million-dollar yacht. Call the manufacturer. Get her in dry dock ASAP. Get the hull fixed."

Tate ground her teeth together. She *really* didn't like hiccups like this. She didn't like messy. She didn't like delays. She didn't like canceling charter reservations. But what choice did she have? Her boat was her bread and butter. If it needed maintenance, it needed maintenance. That's all there was to it.

With a grimace, she nodded. "Set it up. Tell Jones I need to talk to him, eh?"

"Will do." Julio nodded. "It's the right call, Skip."

"It sucks, Julio."

"Yeah, it sucks," he agreed, pulling his cell phone from his hip pocket and leaving to call QRN and set up the repairs.

"Fuck, fuck, fuck," muttered Tate, climbing up the stairs to the bridge and flopping down in her cream leather captain's chair. Out of commission for all of March and most of April? She'd have to cancel at least six charters. What a fucking mess.

It wasn't that Tate couldn't *afford* the time off. Her bank account was flush. Not only had her parents left her a very comfortable inheritance, with which she'd purchased the boat outright, but her business—when she had a *working* vessel—was thriving. It's just that having two months of dead time didn't feel right. How the hell was she supposed to fill those endless days?

Jones knocked twice before sliding the glass door open and stepping inside. "Cap, you need to see me?"

Tate sat up. "I hate to do this to you and the rest of the crew, but ship's got maintenance issues and needs to go into dry dock and maintenance through April."

"You going to rent a sub?"

Tate shook her head. She didn't trust the maintenance on other boats. She wasn't comfortable going out to sea in someone else's ship. "I'll roll over the smaller groups to Uncle Pete, if he's free. The rest I'll try to reschedule with other captains."

"And us?" asked Jones, referring to his staff and that of the boatswain and crew.

She sighed. "I'll pay two months' salary to all of you to cover your contracts."

Jones winced. "Out of your own pocket?"

"It's the right thing to do, Jones. Hoping you'll all come back in May."

"I think you can count on it, Cap." Jones, who was a career steward and twenty-two years older than Tate, nodded. "You're a class act, ma'am."

"Thanks for that, Jones," she said, watching him go.

Pushing away from the console, Tate left the bridge, heading down two flights of stairs to her cabin. Sitting down on her bed, she took a deep breath and sighed.

Eight weeks. Eight weeks off.

What the hell am I going to do for eight weeks? she wondered, looking around the bedroom that she called home.

She could pack a suitcase and stay at Uncle Pete's place, where he kept her childhood bedroom ready and waiting for her. Maybe he could use some help on his charters too—Tate would be glad to lend a hand. It was the least she could do if he was going to cover some of her business.

Glancing at her desk, her eyes landed on her laptop. She reached over, pulled it onto her bed, and opened it. It had been weeks since she'd looked at Facebook or opened her personal e-mail account—she'd been slammed with winter sailfishers, and it was all she could do to keep with messages and reservations that pertained to business—but with a two-month hiatus suddenly and unexpectedly lying before her, time had suddenly slowed down.

Scrolling through dozens of junk e-mails, she stopped when one subject line caught her eye: *Spend St. Patty's at Summerhaven!*

She bit her bottom lip as she eyed the message. Rolling over onto her stomach with her feet in the air, she clicked on it, her heart hammering as she watched the hourglass icon spin, waiting for it to open.

Since leaving Finian at the Druid back in November, she'd tried very hard not to think about him, mostly because it didn't feel good. It stung, and she didn't know what to do with those sharp jabs of pain when she remembered him. Sometimes, she relived their fast and furious love affair in her dreams, however, and she'd wake up slick with longing and tempted to message him over Facebook. It would pass, though, that quick, acute yearning. If she ignored it, it would go away. And as the months sailed by, he faded little by little.

It was just a weekend fling. Don't try to make it more than it was, she reminded herself whenever she did think of him. To pour salt on the wound, he too hadn't gotten in touch over Facebook or Instagram, though both of them had active profiles.

Does he ever look me up? she wondered.

In November and December, she'd checked on him from time to time, gazing at the picture on his profile or smiling at a shot of him holding up Jenny so she could put the star on the top of Ian's Christmas tree. Finally, by January, she'd had to force herself to stop looking. She'd put her laptop away and mostly ignored it since.

Until now.

The message appeared on the screen, and Tate held her breath as she read.

Dear family and friends,

You are cordially invited to spend St. Patrick's Weekend with us at the Summerhaven Event and Conference Center this year!

We will be opening a handful of winterized cottages located on Oxford Row and planning meals and events that will highlight our Irish heritage. Cost will be nominal.

Please let us know if you will be joining us from March 14–18, and we will look forward to honoring our patron saint with you!

Love,

Rory, Brittany, Tierney, Burr, Ian, Hallie, Jenny, & Finian

Finian.

She took a deep breath, filling her lungs.

Sliding her eyes up the screen, she noted that the message had been sent three weeks ago, on February 10, and her lips pursed as she wondered whether or not there would still be space for her.

That is, *if* she decided to attend.

The idea of seeing Britt and Hallie again was compelling, but the idea of seeing Finian again had her stupid heart soaring…which made her snap her laptop closed with a huff.

"You're *not* going," she said softly aloud. "Absolutely not."

As much as she wished she could, Tate couldn't deny the fact that she'd gotten attached to Finian during their weekend together. And going up there for St. Patty's would just reinvigorate her crush, right? Right.

"So you're not going," she muttered. "That's that. Get over him."

Get over him. Hmm. Get over him?

But how *will you get over him if you don't go back up there and find some closure?*

The idea snowballed in her head, the merits of the plan asserting themselves far more loudly than the *dis*advantages.

Here were the facts: since returning from New Hampshire, she hadn't had a date, hadn't screwed around, hadn't fucked, hadn't even kissed a man. Nothing. Nada. She was frozen because every time she contemplated getting physical with someone, she'd think of Fin.

She'd remember some funny thing he said or the way his face looked when he was sleeping. She'd think about the way he'd touched her—gentle, then rough, then gentle again—or the way he'd kissed her. She'd cross her legs remembering how divine it had felt to have his cock full and throbbing inside of her. She'd think about his sisters and brother and wonder if he was a good mechanic. She'd wonder how many he'd fucked since her, and it would make her so sad that her appetite would wane and her lust cool.

And without even meaning to, she'd step back from whatever liaison she was considering.

But maybe…just maybe…she'd idealized him from a distance.

Maybe his eyes and smiles *weren't* as sparkly in real life as they were in her memories.

Maybe he *wasn't* as effortlessly funny.

Maybe the sex *wasn't* as good as she remembered.

Maybe he was just some boy who'd captured her imagination for one sweet, sexy weekend, but her memories were making him into something he wasn't. At any rate, her memories were making it impossible for her to move on.

"So…maybe you *should* go back," she said, opening her laptop again and hitting "reply" before she could play devil's advocate and talk herself out of it. "Go back up there and get him out of your system, Tate."

Hey, Britt,

It's Tate here.

I've been slammed with charters since New Year's, but my schedule just opened up, and if the invitation is still open, I'd love to come for St. Patty's.

Let me know!

She pressed send, then refreshed the screen. Over the next hour, when she should have been rescheduling the charters she needed to cancel, she packed up her belongings and refreshed the screen…over and over and over…until there it was: *RE: Spend St. Patty's at Summerhaven!*

Gulping softly, Tate clicked on the message, rubbing her sweaty hands together and chewing on her bottom lip as it loaded.

Tate, we always have room for you!

See you on the 14th and YAY!!

Britt

"Yes!" she hissed in victory, clapping her hands together.

Yes, said some salty part of her brain that wasn't a bit fooled. It gave her side eyes. It pursed its lips. It called her out on her bullshit. *Good luck with that…closure.*

***

"Ooo! Yay!"

Finian looked up from the long table in the

Summerhaven office where he was folding flyers and stuffing them into envelopes. Across from him, Mrs. Toffle was running the envelopes through a stamp machine, and in an hour, Ian would be back to take bins to the post office before it closed.

"Good news?" he asked Brittany, who was sitting in the adjacent sitting room by the fireplace with her laptop on her lap.

Well…what was *left* of her lap. At almost seven months pregnant, she had more belly than lap at this point.

"Yes!" She looked up and nodded. "One more for St. Patrick's Weekend."

"This late in t' game? Cheeky fucker, whoever it is."

Mrs. Toffle looked up with a gasp and scowled at Fin. "Language, Mr. Kelley!"

"Sorry, Ms. T," he said.

"Though Finian does have a point," she continued, agreeing with him. "The festivities are in two weeks. Surely they could have given you more notice?"

Brittany shrugged. "I don't mind. It's just one more person. Besides, it's Tate! I barely got to visit with her at the wedding, so—"

"Wait!" Finian's neck snapped up. "Wha—*who*?"

Brittany's blue eyes focused on his, surprised by his reaction. "Huh?"

"You, uh…you said…" His tongue darted out, and he licked his lips, trying to ignore the sudden and almost painful hammering of his heart. "Tate's comin'? *Tate*?"

"Yeah. Tate. My friend from camp? Small? Blonde? She was at my wedding. Ringing any bells?"

Fin ignored her sass. "She's comin' *here*?"

"Um. Yeah. For St. Patrick's Weekend." She laughed softly. "You look like you've seen a ghost."

"Maybe just heard about one," he muttered.

Tate.

Feckin' Tate, who left me at the Druid, with my heart bleedin' all over my sleeve.

Feckin' Tate, who, despite my pathetic hopes, hasn't called, hasn't written, hasn't so much as liked *one of the stupid, feckin' clickbait pictures I've posted on Facebook and Instagram in the months since she left.*

Feckin' Tate, who was the hottest feckin' girl I've ever known, who's haunted my bloody dreams near-nightly, makin' me so feckin' horny by mornin', my knob is like to snap off.

That Tate. Was coming back. To Summer-fucking-haven.

And frankly, despite the way his heart had screeched to a halt at the very mention of her name before starting up again like it was off to the damned races, Fin didn't know whether to smile or frown at the prospect of seeing her again. Did he want to kiss her or wring her neck?

It had been a long four months since she left, and respecting her wishes not to reach out to her had been brutal. But she was clear from the beginning—she'd told him: *Don't get attached.* And what had he bloody well done? He'd fallen for her. Well, fine. That was bad enough. He certainly wasn't going to act the eejit, chasing at her heels like a lovesick puppy and wishing he could have her when he couldn't.

Believing that he'd never see her again had been one of the only things making their separation easier. He thought about her a lot, sure, but he also knew that he had an airplane ticket back to Ireland dated March 20, and he'd likely never cross paths with her again. She'd be a distant and sweet memory of a whirlwind weekend in the States, fading with time and eventually releasing whatever unwanted hold she had on his heart.

Now? Knowing that he'd be seeing her again in two weeks? He was thrown. All of the hot, consuming lust he'd been trying to ignore for the last few months came brimming back up to the surface now as Britt and Ms. T discussed which cabin was available for Tate's use. Yeah, he wanted her. On a physical level, he wanted her bad. No, that wasn't true. On *every level*, he wanted her bad, which, frankly, was a problem.

Finian had had plenty of time to think since Tate left, and he'd come to a realization about himself that had initially surprised him: while he didn't want a clingy, uppity lass like Cynthia on his arm, it turned out he wanted something considerably deeper than Tate was willing to offer. With the right girl, he wanted the *possibility* of love. He wanted the *possibility* of commitment. He even wanted the *possibility* of forever.

Love. Commitment. Forever.

Three things that Tate was 150 percent not interested in having or offering. The fact that Finian wanted the possibility of those things with Tate was his problem, not hers.

So regardless of the fact that she looked like an angel and fucked like a demon, he could do them both a favor in two weeks when she arrived at Summerhaven.

He could stay the fuck away from her.

chapter six

"Pick up Tate at t' airport, wouldja, Finian?" he mumbled in a high-pitched, wheedling voice, adjusting and readjusting his sweaty fingers on the steering wheel of a Summerhaven truck. "I need Rory to fuck me some more before we've got a wailin' brat runnin' 'round t' place."

Blowing out an annoyed breath, Fin pressed the brake at a red light and glanced at the GPS. He was minutes away from the Manchester airport, which meant that his plan to stay the fuck away from Tate had pretty much been blown to shite right out of the gate. It wasn't like he could say no to a woman seven and a half months pregnant, now, could he? No. So he'd answered yes. *Yes, Britt, I'll pick her up.* But how was he supposed to avoid Tate when he was about to be trapped in the cab of a pickup with her for the next bloody hour?

And that wasn't even the worst of it. The worst of it was that for the past two weeks, he hadn't been able to think of anything but seeing Tate again. His bloody wanker had been wanked so much, he wondered that he had any cum left in his balls. And he'd been distracted—so fucking distracted—that his cousins had started to notice, happy to give him shite about it because they were all cunts and that was the truth, even though he loved them hard.

"He's not even fluthered, and he's out of it!" observed Rory.

"Are ya knackered after doin' nothin' all day?" asked Ian.

"Nah, he's just got an early bout o' spring fever!" said Tierney.

Ha. The only fever Finian had was the one with Tate Jennings' name on it.

And man, but he fucking hated it.

"Stupid man wantin' what he can't have," he muttered, turning into the airport.

He had a quick choice to make. Did he want to park the car and meet her in the terminal? Or did he want to pull up and wait for her in the arrivals area? He decided on the latter, hoping that it would seem more casual and disinterested than waiting eagerly at the foot of the escalator as she slowly descended. Pulling over to the curb by the baggage claim area, he scanned the sidewalk for her platinum head but didn't see her waiting, which made sense because her flight shouldn't be landing for another five minutes. He cut the engine, hoping the airport police would leave him alone to wait, and checked his reflection in the rearview mirror.

His brown hair was cut short, and he wore a light beard covering his jaw. He had the trademark green Kelley eyes, and a smattering of freckles across his nose.

Yer man looks cla, he thought with grim satisfaction, twisting his neck to see the sliding doors open, then looking away as a businessman exited the airport.

His heart thumped with anticipation as he checked out the clock on the dashboard. 4:35. *She's landing now.*

Reaching for the tuner, he turned on the radio, turning the knob until he settled on "Castle on the Hill," by Ed Sheeran, who, for all that he was born in England, was one quarter Irish through his father, which was good enough for Fin.

Listening to the catchy, U2-style ballad about childhood friends and going home had Fin in a proper reverie, playing drums on the steering wheel and singing along with Ed, when a sharp knock on the passenger-side window made him jump a foot high.

And there she was. A good ten minutes early.

"I miss the way you make me feel, and it's real," sang Ed as Fin stared in surprise at her expectant, slightly amused face.

Opening the door, she grinned at him from the sidewalk. "Ed Sheeran?"

Fin nodded, barely able to get his mind around the fact that he was hearing her voice in person once again.

"Yeah," she said. "He's good. No shame."

He reached for the radio knob and switched it off. "Hi."

"Hi."

Her hair had grown out a bit since he'd last seen her—it was past her shoulders now but as light as ever, with one aqua streak, the exact color of her eyes, framing her face. And it was dead sexy.

"Yer hair's blue."

"Not all of it," she said, a spot of pink appearing on each cheek.

Was she feeling shy around him? Hmm. That'd be new.

"Got a suitcase?"

She nodded.

He slid from his seat and walked around the back of the truck, careful not to make eye contact with her as he took it. Collapsing the handle, he hefted it into the back, then opened his door and climbed into the truck. Next to his hip, she buckled her seat belt.

Turning the key in the ignition, he glanced at her briefly. "Ready to go?"

Her eyes searched his face for a minute, grave in their own way, before she gave him a fake half smile and nodded. "Sure."

"Grand," he snapped, pulling into traffic and pointing north.

***

It wasn't the greeting that Tate had expected.

But then again, what *had* she expected? For him to pull her into his arms and kiss her passionately? For him to say something funny or try to make her laugh or otherwise try to engage with her? For him to make some comment about the fact that they hadn't stayed in touch, but how glad he was to see her?

She wasn't sure, but there was a palpable awkwardness between them that she didn't like at all; especially since Fin had made her feel so comfortable the last time she'd seen him.

See, Tate? You were right! During your time apart, you made him into something he wasn't! You made the right choice to come up here and dispel all the silly longing in your heart! Well done!

Except her pep talk was totally false.

She didn't feel any sense of victory.

And her longing for Fin was as sharp as ever.

But maybe…just maybe…he didn't feel the same about her?

Only one way to find out.

"So…" she started, holding her hands up to the heating vents to warm them, "how have you been?"

"Fine."

A one-word answer. Hmm.

"I've been busy," she offered, when he didn't ask. "I worked nonstop through the holidays and then through January and most of February too." When he didn't respond, she hurried to fill the silence. "How about Summerhaven? Busy there?"

With one hand on the wheel, he shrugged. "Not bad."

Ooo! Two words. Improvement.

"Any big groups? Weddings?"

He stopped at a stoplight and gave her the side eye. "No big groups."

She'd only asked the question to find out about weddings. At some point over the last few months, she'd tried to convince herself that Fin probably chose a different girl at every wedding and fucked around with her. It was one of the ways that Tate had assured herself that she wasn't special to him and should try harder to get over him.

"Um…any weddings?" she asked, her voice uncharacteristically timid.

He was staring straight ahead, but the muscle in his jaw flexed before releasing. "Two since Rory's."

She'd been holding her breath as she waited for him to answer, and now she exhaled, taking a deep breath as she ran a hand through her hair. *Two since Rory's. Hmm.*

It was an interesting combination of words and made

her wonder: Did he want to talk about what had happened at Rory's? He was acting really cool. Almost bitter.

Was he angry with her? But why would he be? She'd never asked for anything. She'd never promised him anything. He didn't have a right to be angry with her…

…no more than she had a right to feel possessive of him and where—or with whom—he'd been spending his time. But it didn't lessen her yearning to know.

"Meet anyone interesting at the other two weddings?"

He cleared his throat. "How about some music?"

Without waiting for her to answer, he reached for the radio knob and turned it to the station he'd been listening to before. A super emo Shawn Mendes song filled the cab of the truck, and Tate huffed softly, turning to stare out the window.

Why was he acting like this?

And maybe more importantly, why did she care?

But fuck. She did. She did, and she hated that she did.

Reaching forward, she turned the radio off, then shifted in her seat to face him.

"Look, I'm not sure what's going on here, but I don't want things to be awkward."

"Then leave the radio on—"

"Fin, come on—"

"—and when we get to Summerhaven, I'll drop you off at Trinity. I'll help you bring your suitcase inside, and then I'll turn around and walk away. And that's how it'll be all weekend. I won't look at you. I won't talk to you. I'll leave you alone…just like you asked me to. Just like you want."

Her bottom lip slipped between her teeth, and she bit on it lightly, considering his words, trying to ignore the way they made her ache with loneliness when she thought about the last time they'd spent the weekend together.

"Turn on the radio," he said softly, the unmistakable color of anger threaded through his tone.

"No," she answered.

"Turn on the radio," he growled.

"No! I don't *want* you to leave me alone."

"Really? Because it felt like you did. Yeah, I'm pretty sure you did. Remember in Boston when you told me not to call?" He paused, clenching his jaw as he stared at the highway. "Turn on the goddamned radio, Tate."

"Please," she said, her heart skipping beats. "I just want to talk to you."

"*Damnú air!* About *what?*" he asked, his tone incredulous. "What the *hell* do you want from me, woman?"

"I want—I just want—I want to—"

He pulled the truck over to the side of the highway, the tires screeching to a stop. "Do you even *know* what you want?"

"I—I just…Why are you so mad at me?"

"Because I had to fight m'self every day not to call you, not to text you, not to message you on goddamn bloody Facebook. Because four months of wantin' someone sucks balls. Because I tried to feckin' forget you!" he cried, shifting his body to stare at her. "And I was almost out of the goddamned bloody woods, and you show up again!"

She gulped, looking at things from his point of view, through his eyes.

"Tell me this, Tate. How come there's one set of rules for me and another for you? I'm not allowed to call or text or reach out after you leave…but *you're* allowed to come back? If I hadn't fucked ya, I'd think you had balls of steel to pull a trick like that."

She stared at him, beyond surprised that her decisions—meant to *keep* them both from any pain—had *caused* so much. "I didn't mean for—"

"What? For one of us to develop actual feelin's?" he said, his green eyes roiling with emotion. "I get it. You don't believe in love. You don't want it. Yer not interested. Fine." He paused only for a moment before continuing that thought. "But I'm not as cold as you, Tate. I fell for you that weekend. I know you told me not to, but I couldn't bloody help it. Stupid Fin. Stupid me." He huffed loudly, banging his hands on the steering wheel. "Anyway, I'm leavin' for Ireland next week. And you're...you're...*impossible.* So let's just stay out of each other's way this weekend, right? We'll just...leave each other alone."

But Tate had meant what she said before: she didn't want Fin to leave her alone. Not to mention, slicing through all of this emotional vomit was an all-consuming need to have her original question answered.

"Were you with anyone? At the other weddings?"

"Fuck," he muttered, staring at the highway. Finally, he turned to her and spat, "No!"

Tate learned that important lesson the moment he said, *No.*

It isn't just bad things that can sucker-punch you.

Good things can knock the wind out of you too.

Maybe she didn't even know the right answer to the question until he gave it. She didn't know why it mattered so much. But it did. And the word *no*, small though it was, was suddenly her favorite word in all the world.

Reaching for his forearm, she rested her fingers tentatively on his brown, wiry hairs for a moment, then curled her fingers, holding onto him, her breathing becoming increasingly jagged and shallow.

"Jaysus, Tate," he whispered, a note of pleading entering his tone. "What do you want from me?"

"I don't know," she said. "I only know that it makes me…happy…that you weren't with anyone."

He didn't look especially pleased by this admission, but he didn't pull his arm away from her either, so it was hard to tell.

"Were you?" he asked, looking deeply into her eyes. "With anyone?"

She shook her head, her voice a whisper. "No."

"I don't know what this is," he admitted softly.

"Me neither," she said. "Feels like unchartered waters."

He tilted his head to the side. "Why did you come back?"

And that part of her brain that had laughed at her two weeks ago when she'd RSVP'd and quickly bought her airline ticket from Marathon to Manchester snickered at her knowingly. *It was, um, closure, wasn't it, dummy?* Except it wasn't. It never had been. It was as simple as this: she wanted—no, she *needed*—to see Finian again, and at the time, she hadn't known how to admit that to herself. But why? The why behind that question still scared the shit out of her.

As though he sensed it was too difficult for her to face the truth of that question, he asked another instead: "Did you think about me?"

She clenched her jaw. Unable to hold the intense eye contact between them, she looked down at her fingers on his arm and nodded.

"You did?"

"Yes." She licked her lips and nodded again, gathering her courage to look up at him. When she did, he reached for her face, tenderly cupping her cheek with his hand.

"I'm leavin' in a few days," he said, scanning her eyes.

"I know," she said. "Me too."

"I like you."

"I know."

"No, Tate," he said. "That's not good enough." He searched her eyes, then repeated, "I like you."

Her breathing was so quick and shallow, she was getting dizzy. To steady herself, she reached up and covered his hand with hers.

"Close your eyes," he said gently.

Gratefully, she closed them, whimpering softly when his lips—as warm and soft and possessive as she remembered them—landed on hers. He kissed her slowly, his lips brushing and nipping like they had all the time in the world instead of just the opposite. Or maybe as though he was savoring the renewed contact as much as she, like his lips had been doing nothing for four months but waiting— not talking, not laughing, not singing, not eating—just *waiting* for the chance to be pressed against hers again.

When he drew away, she kept her eyes closed, but every sense was heightened when he leaned close to her ear and whispered, "*Mo cailleach*, I like you so much."

And Tate, whose lips were no longer her own, took a deep, tremulous breath and formed them to whisper, "I like you too."

His laugh, so soft and surprised, made a hundred

butterflies take flight in her stomach, and she opened her eyes as though he'd commanded it.

"That's my girl."

"*Your* girl?" she asked, still feeling dazed by her admission. She couldn't remember the last time she'd allowed herself to "like" a man she was also kissing, let alone admit it to him.

He laughed again. "Okay, fine. Have it your way. You're not my girl."

Her gaze slid down to his lips. Full and delicious, she wanted them on hers again, and she wanted them there for the foreseeable future, even if that future was only a handful of days.

"*Mo cailleach*, you're an infuriatin', complicated woman. Who told you that likin' someone was all bad?"

"What does that mean?" she asked.

"What? Infuriatin'? Frustratin'. Difficult. Aggrava—"

"I know what infuriating means," she said. She gave him a look as she wound her fingers through his and lowered their hands to the vinyl seat between them. "Mo kay-leech. What's that mean?"

He winced, then licked his lips. "You won't like it."

Her heart started beating faster. Did it mean something sappy and sentimental that would have her throwing up in her mouth? She braced herself, fighting her facial muscles against an imminent grimace. "Does it mean 'love' or 'sweetheart' or something else like that?"

"Eh, *no*. It's hard to translate. I mean…well, literally, it means…'hag,' but I'm not callin' you a hag, now! It's a queer word that has secondary meanin's about a woman bein' a sorceress or a…"

Her mind acknowledged that he was still talking, but she had stopped listening, her lips tilting up into a smile, a laugh starting in her belly, bubbling up through her chest, passing her heart en route to her throat, which opened with unexpected joy as the sound burst forth into unruly giggles.

"You've been c-calling me a—a—a—hag?"

Unable to stop laughing, she stared at him, utterly besotted and totally unable to look away. And if Tate *had* been a woman who didn't believe in love a scant few months ago, she couldn't be certain that she didn't believe in it now. If he'd been calling her "sweetheart" or "honey" or "love" in Irish, it would have been hard for her to accept, but this man, who somehow read her perfectly without even knowing the complicated, hidden, secret language of her frightened heart, had been—affectionately—calling her a hag. It was perfect. It was *beyond* perfect.

It was, though there was no way Tate would have acknowledged it even if she'd realized it for herself, the moment she fell in love with him.

He stared back at her like she was completely nuts. "Uh, yeah? You like that, uh, that nickname, huh? But like I said, it doesn't mean the same thing in—"

"Fin."

"Yeah?"

"Shut up," she said, clenching the muscles that were demanding his cock, hard and throbbing, deep inside of her.

"Yeah."

"I need to be in your bed...*now.*"

"Now now?"

"*Now* now."

"Right," he said, putting both hands on the steering

wheel, shifting the car into drive and iron-footing the gas as he merged back onto the quiet highway with a squeal of tires. "Don't take this the wrong way, Tate, because you know I like you, but I think you may be a bit daft."

She nodded, crossing her legs tight in an effort to assuage the ache between her thighs. "I think you might be right."

chapter seven

It was the light through the cottage window that woke Finian, bright in its morning glory, shining down on the angelic head of the woman he'd fucked senselessly for about six straight hours last night.

He'd had her on top and astride, in the shower, and on the edge of the bed. He'd held her in his arms as she sat impaled on his lap, and he'd smacked her naughty fanny as he drilled her from behind. From the moment they'd arrived back at Summerhaven, they'd made up for four months of lost time, and by midnight, they were both aching and exhausted.

And happy.

So fucking happy it should have scared him to death, but it didn't. A man who's been lost in the desert doesn't worry he's drinking too much when someone finally offers him water. He just drinks his fucking fill and then he drinks a little more.

Turning onto his side, he felt his cock twitch then jump, his balls tightening as he stared at her. Tugging on the white sheet just a little, he bared her breasts, watching in fascination as her nipples puckered into tight points. She had several hickeys on the otherwise pristine flesh of both breasts—places where he'd sucked too hard—and the marks on her skin made him even harder.

He leaned forward, running his tongue around one tan areola, his breath whispering over the dark bud that beckoned his lips. She moaned softly as he sucked the sweet nub of warm flesh into his mouth, his tongue bathing her skin as her hands found his head, her fingers threading into his hair and pulling.

Maneuvering between her legs, he licked a path to her other breast as he reached beneath her, clutching the twin globes of her ass as he sucked the left nipple into the wet heat of his mouth. She whimpered his name softly, and he pulled her forward, lining up his cock at the entrance of her pussy.

"Open yer eyes, *mo cailleach.*"

The fluttered open slowly, her eyebrows knitting together in dreamy desire as she stared up at him.

"Do you want me?" he asked.

She arched her back, welcoming the tip of his erection into her hot, soaked sex.

"Say it," he insisted.

"I want you," she said, her voice sleepy and low, her eyes closing as he held her tightly and slid forward slowly, inch by perfect inch, until he was balls deep inside of her, the walls of her pussy clenching tightly around his cock.

He didn't know what was happening between them. He didn't necessarily understand why *this* woman, who tried to appear as though she needed no one, had so captured his attention and his heart, but it was one of those things he could neither explain nor completely understand. He only knew that being with her—being *intimate* with her—was a high he'd never known, and being apart from her for four months had been a low he'd just as soon never revisit again.

"Tate," he murmured, withdrawing his cock to the tip, then surging forward again, "you feel…fuck, but you feel so good."

"Mm-hm," she hummed. "Harder, Fin. Faster. I need…please, I need…"

"You need to come, lass," he said, panting, feeling his own orgasm imminent.

Digging his fingers into her ass, he pulled her impossibly closer, keeping his thrusts short and fast as she whimpered and moaned beneath him. He held her body with one arm as he licked his fingers, then slid them between the delicate folds of her slickened skin to find and tease her clit.

She threw her forearm over her closed eyes, her whole body going rigid for just a second before she cried out his name and the walls of her sex rippled in waves—clench, release, clench, release, clench release clenchreleaseclenchreleaseclenchrelease…

"FUCK!" he growled, his massaged cock swelling thick within her, tight to the point of pain, and then—cresting, cresting, sucking his breath from his lungs—letting go. He groaned in satisfaction, his breath catching as he came inside of her in sweet, hot, glorious pulses of pleasure.

Panting and sweating, he rolled to his back, taking her with him. She sprawled over his chest, her face against his neck, her lips resting on his throat.

"I missed you," he said softly, as the world stopped spinning and he opened his eyes slowly. "Fuck, but I missed you, woman."

He felt her inhalation of breath, and the way she held it before finally letting it go.

"I know," she said softly, her voice like gravel.

It bruised his heart a little that she didn't return the sentiment, but instead of swallowing that small pain, he decided to face it.

"That's not good enough," he said, repeating the same words he'd used in the car last night when she'd had trouble telling him that she liked him.

Disengaging their bodies, Tate rolled to her side, presenting him with her back, and though it took Fin and a moment to realize it, a soft, shuttering breath clued him in to the fact that she was crying.

Tate.

Was crying.

Shite.

He reached for her and pulled her back against his chest gently but firmly, sliding one arm under her head and draping the other over her waist and flattening it beneath her breasts.

"Shhh. Shhh, now, sweet girl. I don't mean to push you so hard," he murmured, holding her tightly and letting her cry. As much as he could, he wanted to absorb the pain she held inside, to reverse her belief that love was impossible, and that caring for someone meant heartache. "What happened to you, lass? What hurts so much, *mo cailleach?*"

"H-Hag," she mewled softly, accompanied by a little chortle crossed with a sniffle.

"I told you that it didn't mean—"

"Shut up, Fin," she said with another sniffle, followed by a deep, jagged breath that filled her lungs, but not without effort. "I like it."

She turned in his arms, facing him with glistening eyes

and damp cheeks, and he *very sternly* told himself that this was *not* a good time to be distracted by the rasp of her still-erect nipples against his chest.

He stared into her eyes, forcing his concentration to zero in on her heart and her head and, just for now, not on her body.

She took another ragged breath and let it go, exhaling against his chest in a puff of warm wind.

"Talk to me," he said. "Let me in just a little."

Her eyes were bleak as she looked at him, a tear slipping from her lashes and sliding down her cheek.

"Please, Tate," he coaxed.

"Stop looking at me," she said softly.

He nodded, rolling to his back. She rested her cheek over his heart, and he stroked her back, waiting for her to talk, trying to be patient.

Finally, when she was ready, she cleared her throat. "I don't *do* this. I don't get emotional. I don't get attached. I don't let people in. Never."

"I know," he said. "But it's okay. You're safe with me."

"Am I?"

And he didn't have to think. He spoke from the heart. "You are."

"I think I only let myself fall for you because everything was temporary."

He knew this. He knew it, and yet he hated to hear it. Her reminder that everything they shared was temporary, in fact, almost ruined the thrill of her inadvertently admitting that she'd fallen for him. Almost.

"Doesn't have to be," he said, purposely keeping his voice light. "We're adults who earn money. I heard about this new invention called an airplane. We don't have to say good-bye forever."

Her lips pressed against his chest for a moment. "Yes, we do. I live in Florida. You live in Ireland. Temporary is why this works."

Fin didn't agree with her. When they'd first met in November, he'd been of the same mind, but as days apart turned into agonizing weeks turned into almost unbearable months, he'd realized that they'd forged a deeper connection in their few days together. And now that they'd reconnected? The idea of losing her again felt...well, terrible. Not that he knew what to do about it. For now, he simply decided not to fight with her.

"We don't have to decide all of that right this minute," he said. "Tell me about you."

"Me." She exhaled loudly, like she couldn't stand the story she was about to tell. "Poor little Tate."

"How's that?"

Her index finger moved absentmindedly over his right pec as she spoke, drawing small circles, one after the other. "When I was eight, we lived in Boston. Me and my parents. One night—a completely boring night in March—my parents hired a sitter and went out to dinner. A date night. Nothing extraordinary. Nothing crazy. Dinner and a movie. Except it was sleeting when they got out of the movie. On the way home, a drunk driver slammed into their car. If the roads hadn't been so slippery, he might have been able to stop, but between his poor reflexes and the weather, he couldn't."

Fin closed his eyes and clenched his jaw. He knew the rest of the story without asking, and it explained so much about her—why she was so closed to love, why she was so certain it would hurt her.

"They were probably killed instantly," she murmured, then added in a barely audible whisper: "Probably."

Fin gulped, his fingers stilling on her back as he processed the terrible thing that had happened to her at such a young age.

"I was sent to live with my Uncle Pete, my mom's older brother, who lived—well, *lives*—in the Florida Keys. He was forty. A bachelor. I barely knew him. He never wanted kids, never wanted to be a father."

"What happened then?" asked Fin, wondering if this "Uncle Pete" had mistreated her in any way, everything inside of him ready to buy a plane ticket to Florida and beat the shite out of the old bastard with his bare hands if that was the case.

"He learned how," she said softly, her voice uncharacteristically vulnerable. "He...became my everything. Mother. Father. Uncle. Family. Friend." She paused for a second, and Fin relaxed, his hand moving gently on her back again. "We were an odd couple, Uncle Pete and me, but he loved me. *Loves* me. And I...well, you know."

He *did* know. She loved him, this uncle who'd taken in a shattered child and given her a safe harbor in the middle of a deadly storm.

"You love him back."

Her finger on his chest stilled, and he realized—yet again—that the word *love* was a painful trigger for her. He rephrased his words: "He's important to you."

"He's all I've got," said Tate, her finger resuming its circles.

Finian almost corrected her. He almost said, *No, sweet girl, you have me too*. But it wasn't the right time for such a declaration. While she was sharing her story, it was his job to listen.

"Was your childhood ever…happy again?"

"I don't know." She took another deep breath, but this one was strong and smooth. "My childhood was like a broken mirror. Fractured glass gives a strange reflection, you know?"

"You were broken."

She nodded. "I'll *always* be broken. That's why…that's why I can't…why I won't…"

"That's why you won't be loved," he finished for her.

"Yes."

Or love in return.

The unspoken words hovered between them for a moment before fading away. It was futile to say them aloud or insist on them, silly to try to make her understand that broken things could be pieced back together with patience and determination, love and time.

And frankly, Finian had no right to say anything.

Fin could practice patience when he wanted to. And when he set his mind to something, he could be very determined. But love? He hadn't loved Cynthia, and he didn't know if he loved Tate. He was infatuated, yes, and he cared about her, certainly, but *love*? The sort of strong, forever, no-matter-what kind of love that a broken girl would need? He didn't know if he had that sort of love to offer her. And besides, they barely had any time to find out. Today was Friday, and she left for home on Monday. Two days later, he'd return to Dublin.

It made him feel heavy hearted.

It made him wish for the sort of time that would allow him to develop the kind of love she needed.

This wasn't supposed to be complicated, he thought to himself. *How did random sex at a wedding turn into something that mattered so much?*

With her cheek on his heart, and his mind whirling with questions, they lay in silence as the world awakened outside of Trinity Cottage, as the finches and chickadees called for their breakfasts. The distant roar of a motor told Fin that his cousin Ian was up and moving, which made Finian muse on a more immediate problem.

They'd been so hungry for time alone with one another, they hadn't even stopped to say hello to the rest of the Havens last night, a choice he and Tate would likely pay for this morning with a hearty round of teasing at breakfast.

"My cousins are goin' to be cunts about this," he said.

"About us sleeping together?" she asked.

"Mm-hm."

She leaned up on his chest, her face lighter and, he thought, more open since telling him about her childhood. It made his stupid heart swell to see it.

"I couldn't give two shits," she answered.

"When you sweet talk like that," said Fin, grinning at her, "I want to fuck you all over again, woman."

"Don't you mean 'hag'?" she asked, letting him flip her to her back and welcoming him by spreading her legs.

"Yeah, I do," he said, grinning at her as his cock stiffened to stone, seeking entry. "*Mo cailleach.* My pretty little witch. I want you."

"I want you too," she said, staring into his eyes.

76

She arched her back, gasping as he slid into her body in one smooth thrust, her ankles rising to lock on his ass, and her eyes rolling back in ecstasy.

And Finian, who now understood the fierce reservations of her heart, held her tightly as he joined his body with hers, desperately hoping that whatever attachment they'd developed for one another wouldn't leave them both forever scarred when it was severed.

***

While Ian, Rory, Finian, Burr, and most of the other guests headed down to the Gilford Ice Arena for a game of hockey, Hallie invited the younger ladies—a very pregnant Brittany, Tate, and Tierney—to her apartment for an afternoon of board games in front of the fire. But games had been quickly abandoned for talking, and it was only a matter of minutes until they asked Tate what was going on between her and Finian.

Contrary to what Fin had predicted, no one had bothered them at breakfast, during a morning hike up West Rattlesnake Mountain, or during lunch, which had featured delectable Irish fare like fish and chips and shepherd's pie. It was almost as though someone had forbidden the heckling of Tate and Finian, which made Tate wonder.

But perhaps strangest of all, as the hours wore on, Tate found that she was *dying* to talk about it—about Finian, about her confusing feelings, about the future or lack thereof. It was such a change for her to actually *want* to talk about a guy, to know that she liked him and he meant something to her, no matter how temporary or unusual their relationship.

"It was so nice of Suzanne to take the girls to the

game," said Hallie, who was nestled into the couch beside Brittany, their slippered feet resting on the coffee table. "Bridey and Jenny are crazy about each other. And it gives *us* a chance to catch up."

"Does Jenny *like* hockey?" asked Tate, thinking that Hallie's little girl seemed awfully young to enjoy the game.

"I don't think she understands it," said Hallie, "but she *loves* Ian. There is, literally, no scenario in which she passes up the chance to spend time with him."

"Does it ever make you jealous?" asked Tierney, who was curled up in a cozy armchair by the fire. "How close Jenny is to my brother?"

Hallie shook her head, a peaceful smile on her lips. "Nope. I love it. They're like two peas in a pod. I don't know if there's anything on earth that makes me happier than seeing Ian and Jenny together."

"Ian's a great dad," agreed Brittany in a dreamy voice. As soon as she realized what she'd said, however, she cut her eyes to Hallie. "Oh, gosh! Not that he's her father...I just meant—"

"I know what you meant," said Hallie. "And it's true. He *is* a great dad to her. In fact..." She scrunched up her nose. "Oh, God...I'm not supposed to tell you girls something that I really, really want to tell you!"

"Well," said Tate, who was sitting in a matching armchair across from Tierney, "now you *have* to tell us."

"You don't want to piss off a woman as pregnant as I am!" Brittany threw a pillow at her friend. "*Spill. It.*"

Hallie flicked a nervous glance at Tierney, then took a deep breath. "You know how we're having a little *céilí* in the barn tomorrow night?"

"What's a *céilí*?" asked Tate.

"A dance," said Tierney. "Like a square dance, but for Irish people."

"Keep going!" insisted Britt.

"Well…there's a priest coming, you know. He's a friend of the boys, and so we were thinking that during the *céilí*," said Hallie, still staring Tierney with a nervous expression, "Ian and I might…"

"Oh, my God!" cried Britt. "Are you getting *married* tomorrow?"

"We were thinking about it," said Hallie, wincing at Tierney. "Are you mad, Tierney?"

Tierney was smiling from ear to ear. "Mad? Why in God's name would I be mad?"

"Because *you* were next to get married," said Hallie. "I would never, ever want to steal your thunder!"

"Oh, Hallie," said Tierney, "I'm only too glad for Ian to go before me. Besides, our wedding isn't until summer!"

"Really? You're sure?"

Tierney nodded. "I promise! I'm so happy for you two!"

Hallie jumped up to hug her almost sister-in-law, and the ladies talked briefly about how they could help Hallie tomorrow.

At one point, Tate glanced around the room, her eyes landing on Brittany, who was staring back at her with a curious expression.

"I can't stand it anymore," Britt blurted out.

"What can't you stand?" asked Tate.

Britt looked at Hallie with a desperate expression. "I know you made us all promise not to ask. And I know you said that Ian would personally beat up anyone who bothered Tate about Finian, but…but…but…I'm *dying* to know, and he wouldn't hit a pregnant lady, would he? No! *Never!* So I figure I'm the *only one* who can ask!" Without waiting for Hallie to answer, Brittany locked eye with Tate. "*What the hell is going on with you two?*"

Tate stared back at her childhood friend—at the wild expression in her pretty blue eyes—and surprised herself by bursting into giggles. "Oh, my God, Britt. You're a junkie for romance!"

Hallie and Tierney joined Tate in laughter, but it quickly faded, and Tate was met with three sets of eyes staring at her with blatant curiosity.

She sighed. "Fine. What do you want to know?"

They all started talking at once, but Brittany yelled, "I was the only one with the courage to ask! I get to go first!" She turned to Tate. "Did it start at my wedding?"

"Yes."

"Did you guys have sex?" asked Hallie.

Tate nodded. "Uh…yeah."

Tierney gasped. "Were you having sex after the wedding? We couldn't find you two anywhere!"

"Roger that. In the choir room at the church."

"Dirty girl!" exclaimed Brittany with dancing eyes. "And last night?"

"Mm-hm." *Lots.* "He stayed overnight with me at Trinity."

"I noticed he didn't come home last night," said Hallie, who was sitting closest to Tate. "You like him, Tate?"

Taking a deep breath, Tate nodded. "I like him."

Britt hit Hallie with a pillow. "I have *never* heard her say that! Despite all of my efforts to find her a boyfriend at camp!"

"That's because she never has," said Hallie.

"So what comes next?" asked Tierney, her expression thoughtful.

"I don't know," answered Tate honestly, her heart pinching a little. "He lives in Ireland. I live in Florida."

"They've got these things called airplanes…" said Tierney.

"Oh, my God!" exclaimed Tate, her eyes widening at Fin's cousin. "You two are definitely related!"

"Did he say the same thing?"

"Verbatim."

"Well, what about it?" asked Britt. "I mean…you could go there and visit him. He could go to Florida to visit you. There's Facebook and Instagram and e-mail and Skype. It's, like, not the worst time in history to be in a long-distance relationship, Tate."

What Brittany said made sense to Tate, and in yet another strange realization, she found that she wasn't totally repelled by the idea of making her "thing" with Fin less than temporary, though that was probably because of the buffer between them: an *ocean*.

"Tate," said Hallie, whose parents had been friends with Tate's in Boston before they died. "They'd want you to be happy. You know that, don't you?"

"Do you remember them, Hallie?"

She nodded. "I do. My mom and your mom were good friends. You came to all of my birthday parties, and they would talk and laugh all afternoon."

"Don't forget me!" said Brittany. "I was there too!"

"But your mom stopped coming after the divorce," said Hallie.

Britt shrugged. "True."

"Oh, my gosh!" said Tierney. "That's right! I almost forgot. Your mothers attended Summerhaven together, didn't they?"

The other three women nodded.

"We're legacies," said Hallie.

"Don't change the subject," snapped Britt, pointing a finger at Tate. "You and Fin. What's the *plan*, Tate? You're *killing* me."

"So dramatic," said Hallie, rolling her eyes. "Leave Tate alone."

"Maybe Tate doesn't know the plan," said Tierney, her green eyes so like Fin's as she watched Tate from across the small sitting room. "Maybe she's still figuring it out."

Grateful for Tierney's gentle understanding, Tate nodded. "This is a first for me, girls. I can't remember the last time I *let* someone like me and actually liked them back. And who do I choose? A man from across the sea. I'm hopeless."

"No, you're not," said Tierney. "You're cautious. I understand that."

"We can't always choose," said Hallie. "Sometimes it just…happens."

"And when it does," added Brittany, "all you can do is hang on."

Her three friends started talking about Hallie's miniwedding tomorrow, and the conversation shifted, but Tate was left with Britt's words resonating in her brain and the idea that maybe—just maybe—she would.

chapter eight

It has been a perfect day, thought Finian, lying on his back in Tate's bed.

To his right, a naked Tate slept beside him, curled up against his side with her head resting on his shoulder and her breath falling on the base of his throat in soft, even whispers. Leaning over just a touch, his lips brushed against her temple and rested there as he thought about Ian and Hallie's surprise wedding, and how it had made him feel to see his cousin get married.

He knew that it was typical for the single men at a wedding to feel a certain amount of panic when watching one of their comrades surrender to marriage, but Fin, standing with Rory, Brittany, Tierney, Burr, and the rest of their friends and family as witnesses, discovered that all *he'd* felt was an unexpected twinge of longing.

And all he could think, as he'd held Tate against his chest with his arms around her waist, was that maybe— someday—he'd like to take the plunge too.

Because she'd had her back to his front, he hadn't been able to see her face as Ian and Hallie exchanged their vows, but what surprised him the most was that she hadn't untangled herself from his arms or otherwise tried to run away from him during the impromptu wedding. And it hadn't even *occurred* to Fin to let her go and stand respectfully beside her. It was only when he caught Tierney watching him with a soft smile on her lips that he'd realized he was resting his chin on Tate's shoulder like they'd been a couple for years.

How strange that he should have attended two weddings with Tate at this point and slept with her more times than he could count on two hands, but he hadn't even spent a week in her presence. Why should she mean so much to him? And what the hell was he supposed to do about it?

As he watched Ian pledge his undying and eternal love to Hallie, he'd had a sudden flashback to the first time he'd met Tate: at Rory and Brittany's rehearsal dinner. His chair had smacked the ground as he'd stood up that night, and when she'd stood up a few minutes later, hers had done the same. If Finian believed in fairies and legends—mind, he wasn't totally certain that he didn't—he might wonder if a spell had been cast, somehow binding him to this strange, standoffish woman and her to him in return.

Tate stirred in her sleep, sighing against him and snuggling closer, and Fin adjusted his grip around her, holding her a little tighter in his arms.

She'd gotten under his skin, and when they said good-bye tomorrow, it was going to ache. Nah. It was going to hurt like a bloody bitch, and Lord only knew for how long. After their first weekend together, he hadn't shaken his longing for her after four months. This weekend, she'd been so much softer and more open to him; it was going to hurt worse this time, and it was going to take even longer to get over her.

"Ah, Tate," he whispered. "I wish things were different, lass."

"Hmm?" she hummed.

He kissed her temple again, lingering, closing his eyes to inhale the light scent of her shampoo mixed with their recent lovemaking.

*Love*making.

Is that what it was?

He clenched his jaw, kissing her again before resting the back of his head on her pillow. What he felt for her was more intense than anything he'd ever felt for another woman, but he still wasn't ready to label it. And all he wished was that he had the time and space to get to a place where he *was* ready.

"Fin?" she whispered.

"I'm here," he said.

"Was I asleep?"

"You were, darlin'," he said. "For a little bit."

"It was a busy weekend," she said. "And you've kept me up two nights in a row."

"Any complaints?" he asked, rolling to his side so he could face her.

She shook her head, her eyes dark and lazy. "None."

"I'll drive you to the airport tomorrow," he said, leaning up on his elbow.

"Oh," she murmured, looking away from him. "Okay."

Fuck. He didn't mean to wreck the mood. He was just so damned sad and confused and fucked up about letting her go and never seeing her again.

"I wish we had more time," he said.

Her eyes cut to his. "You do?"

"I do." He paused, wondering how much he should say, desperate not to push her away but well aware that his time with her was running down. "I don't know what this is. On one hand, I barely know you, but on the other, I've known you for months and all I want is…more time. Feckin' bites that there's none left."

"I could stay," said Tate in a small voice, "for a few extra days."

"You could? You'd do that?"

She shrugged. "My ship's in dry dock until the first week of May. I told my Uncle Pete I'd give him a hand with some of his upcoming charters, but I don't think he'd mind if I stayed until Wednesday. That's when you're leaving, right?"

The wind was knocked out of him. He couldn't believe that she was offering him more time. It was like a reprieve from execution at this point, and he pulled her into his arms, kissing her soundly.

"That's when I'm leavin'," he said, grinning at her as he nipped the corners of her lips, his cock swelling with the news that it could invade her sweet body numberless times between now and Wednesday evening.

"I'll change my flight in the morning," she said.

"Whatever will we do until then?" asked Fin.

Tate put her hands on his shoulders and pushed him to his back, then straddled his chest, firmly gripping the base of his rigid cock, then sinking down on it with a satisfied groan.

"More of this," she suggested.

He reached for her breasts, teasing her nipples until she whimpered. Then clutching her hips, he controlled the way she slid back and forth on his slick cock until they came together in breathless pants of "fuck" and "yes" and "Fin" and "Tate" and the kind of soft, happy laughter that is only present when you have—for a few blissful moments—discovered that everything you were about to lose is still yours for the taking.

***

Tate swatted at her nose, the sound of buzzing making her semiconscious mind believe that a fly or bee had invaded her love nest.

Buzz. Buzz, buzz, buzz.
Buzz. Buzz, buzz, buzz.
CRASH!

Her eyes popped open, and she sat up in bed.

Beside her, Finian lay on his stomach with his naked—and incredibly tight—ass in the air. She grinned at the matching fingernail marks she'd left on the twin globes before pulling the sheets and comforter over his sleeping body.

Buzz. Buzz, buzz, buzz.

Looking over the side of the bed, she found her cell phone—the guilty party—scooting around the floor like a Mexican jumping bean with a constant stream of buzzing noises and accompanying vibrations.

Hmm, she thought, reaching down for it. *It buzzed for so long that it buzzed itself off the table? What's going on?*

Sitting up with her feet dangling over the side of the bed, she turned the phone over. *Frank Sturgess.* Frank. Uncle Pete's best friend. What the hell?

"Hello? Frank?"

"Tate! Oh, thank God! Tate."

Her blood went cold. Cold as ice. And it actually

occurred to her, as her breath caught in her throat, to throw the phone across the room and shatter it so she wouldn't have to hear whatever was coming next.

Instead she gulped. "F-Frank?"

"Um. Something happened. It's Pete."

"No," she said, her voice firm and insistent. "It *isn't* Pete."

"Tatey? You gotta listen to me, honey. Your uncle's in the hospital."

She couldn't breathe, and the room was spinning like mad. "He's dead."

The phone slipped from her hand, smacking on the floor and waking up Fin. "Tate?"

She sat on the edge of the bed, naked and frozen, the faraway voice of her uncle's best friend calling her name. "Tate? Tatey, you there? Tate? Let me explain what happened! Tate?"

Fin sat up. "What's goin' on?"

But she couldn't speak. She couldn't move. She couldn't breathe, or swallow, or see. She closed her eyes against the spinning of the room, her head going dim and dizzy. *It's happening again. You're alone. You're going to be all alone.*

"Tate? Who's—?" Fin leaned over her, reaching down for her phone and bumping it against her elbow. When she didn't take it, he cleared his throat. "Hello? Uh, this is, uh, Tate's friend, Finian. She's, uh…ah. Oh, yes. I see. Mmm. When? Right. Last night." He paused for a moment, and Tate squeezed her eyes tighter. "Uh-huh. I'll tell her. Right-o. Huh. So he's—? Well, that's good, ain't it? Yeah. Yeah. Right. Okay. She's, uh…she's a bit shaken up, sir. Mm-hm. She'll call you back. Right. Good. Bye, then."

Fin must have positioned his body behind hers, because the next things she knew, she was drawn back against his chest, and his arms were around her.

"Darlin'," he said. "Can you hear me?"

She clenched her jaw so hard she wondered if it was possible to break it.

"I'll take that as a yes," he said, his voice soft and very, very close to her ear. He held her tighter. "Listen to me. Yer uncle's not dead. Do you hear me? He's alive, Tate. He's *not* dead."

He's alive, Tate. He's not dead.

If she'd been standing up, she would have collapsed under the weight of her intense relief, but because Finian was holding her so tight, all she could do was fall back against him, her naked body slumping into his, her rigid muscles loosening to jelly, her eyes burning with a sudden and brutal onslaught of tears.

Her body shook with the force of her sobs, and she reached up to hold on to the arms he had—like steel bands—around her body. She held on to him and cried until she was weak from the effort, and Finian lay back, taking her with him, spooning her against his body, holding her tightly.

"Tell me when you're ready to hear more," he said softly.

"T-Tell m-me," she sobbed.

"He had a heart attack yesterday evenin' at the, uh, the Waterin' Can?"

"W-Watering *C-Crab*."

"Yeah, right. Fell off his barstool clutchin' at his chest. That bloke on the phone went with him to the hospital, and they confirmed it was a heart attack." He paused for a moment. "But he's all right, Tate. He's restin'. He's goin' to be okay."

Her mind focused to one inviolate and uncompromising thought.

I need to go to Uncle Pete.

Grasping at Fin's hands, she pulled them away from her body, half sliding, half lunging from the bed. She tore open the dresser drawers, throwing her clothes on the bed, and whipped open the armoire to grab her suitcase, unzip it, and lay it open on the floor.

"Tate, love, slow down," said Finian, sitting up in bed.

"Don't tell me what to do," she snapped, pulling a bra from the pile on the bed and fastening it into place before yanking on some panties. She ran to the bathroom and returned a moment later, clutching everything she'd brought in her arms.

"Tate, it's six in the mornin'."

"And I'm sure there's a flight leaving for somewhere in Florida by seven," she said, without flicking a glance at him. "I intend to be on it."

She threw all of her toiletries into the open suitcase, then put her arms around the clothes on the bed and added them too. Grabbing a pair of possibly dirty jeans, she pulled them on, then jerked her phone, cord and all, from the wall beside the bed and threw it in her purse.

"Can you slow down, lass?"

"No. I can't," she bit back, finally sparing a look for him. He looked so confused, so worried and upset that she felt—deep inside—the awful feeling of caring for someone and letting them down, but she didn't have time for Fin right now, so she squelched it. "Get dressed. I need a ride."

"You heard me, right? He's okay," said Fin. "He's goin' to be okay."

"He's lying in a fucking hospital bed, Finian! He had a heart attack! A fucking heart attack! He's *not* okay. He's a *long way* away from okay!" She knelt on the floor, about to zip up the suitcase when she realized she was only wearing a bra on top. Pulling out the balled-up black T-shirt that she'd worn on Friday, she wiggled into it, then zipped the case shut. "Are you driving me or not?"

He swung his legs over the side of the bed and leaned down for his shirt and pants. "I'm drivin' you."

As she waited for him to dress, she took out her phone again and scrolled through her messages. Frank had called eight times before she'd finally picked up. *Fuck. Fuck, fuck, fuck. What if Pete had died?* What if she'd had a chance to see him one last time and she had missed that chance?

Finian stood next to her, bracing his hand on the bedpost as he pulled on his shoes. "I'll go get the truck and come back for you."

She nodded curtly, swiping at the tears on her cheeks. Was she crying? Apparently, she was.

He reached for her face, presumably to kiss her or comfort her, but she didn't want him right now. She wanted to be with Uncle Pete. She jerked away from Fin, crossing her arms over her chest. He drew back as though slapped, and the look in his eyes hurt her, but she just didn't have time for his hurt feelings right now.

Uncle Pete. I need to get to Uncle Pete. Now.

"I'll be right back," he said softly, leaving her alone.

And Tate, who had tried so fucking desperately since the death of her parents to stay clear of anything that could remotely hurt her as badly as their loss, realized that she'd done a very poor job of achieving her mission. Pain was a part of life. There was no escaping it. There was no denying it. There was no way to avoid it. And it was so fucking unfair, it made her feel eight years old all over again.

So she did what any frightened child would do: she sat down on the bed, and she wept.

***

Finian understood Tate's reaction to her uncle's illness.

He completely understood.

Back at home, Fin had a mate, Trevor, who was originally from Belfast and had been a kid there during the Troubles before moving south to Dublin. And anytime there were fireworks or a car backfired, he'd clutch at his head, and his eyes would dart around wildly for a second while he looked for a place to hide.

It was called PTSD, post-traumatic stress disorder, and no matter how many shrinks Trev had visited, they'd all said the same: meds and therapy would help, but there was no cure for PTSD, only healing.

And his Tate? She'd looked just like Trevor, sitting on the side of the bed, frozen in terror, waiting to hear the words she'd dreaded since the day she'd lost her parents: that someone else she loved was dead.

Even now, sitting beside him in the truck as he drove her back down to Manchester, he wondered if she'd ever gotten any help. At this point, he had nothing to lose, so he decided to ask her.

"When you were little," he started, "you said yer uncle didn't know how to be a parent."

"He did his best," she said, her tone defensive.

"I know he did," said Fin, treading lightly, "and I know you love him for it. But what I'm wonderin' is…did he get you help for it?"

"He adopted me."

"Right. But did he get you a therapist? Someone to help you grieve?"

She didn't answer, and when Fin glanced at her, her jaw was set and her arms were crossed tightly over her chest.

"I'm not criticizin' him," said Fin gently. "I'm sayin' that you were traumatized at a young age, and I'm wonderin' who helped you see yer way through it."

"Uncle Pete," she muttered.

"Yer uncle, who had no idea how to be a parent to a little girl."

"Shut up, Fin," she said, her voice like gravel.

"It's never too late," he went on. "My mate, Trev, is still workin' through the Troubles."

"The Troubles?"

"Yeah. In, uh, Northern Ireland? He grew up on the northwest side of Belfast where they had years of bombin' and the like. Saw too many terrible things for a wee one. Still crouches down when a loud noise surprises him." He paused for a second. "You did that this mornin' when yer uncle's friend called."

"I didn't crouch."

"No. You froze. You froze out of fear."

"Are you a doctor? A psychiatrist?" she snapped, turning to glare at him.

He stopped at a red light and met her furious eyes with his. "No, lass. I'm just a dumb paddy who cares somethin' fierce for you."

Physically, she crumpled. Her head drooped forward, and he heard her harsh intake of breath, more a twisted sob than anything else. Her shoulders shook and instead of crossing her arms, he realized she was holding them. She was hugging herself. Maybe because when she'd been so little and so alone, there'd been no one else to do it for her.

Pulling the car over, Finian unbuckled his seat belt and hers, gripped her upper arms firmly, and drew her body against his. He held her tightly, rubbing her back and whispering soothing words in Irish. She cried against his shoulder until the fabric was soaked and she was hiccupping every few seconds.

"I'm a mess," she said. "A fucking…mess."

"Nah, Tate. Yer trapped," he said, rubbing her back. "When somethin' bad happens, yer eight years old again, just like the second a car backfires, Trev is back in Belfast."

"Is therapy h-helping your f-friend?" she asked through sniffles.

He realized that she'd relaxed against him, and he savored the moment, knowing that it was likely his last chance to hold her. "I think so, yeah. Can't hurt, right?"

She sniffled again. "Sorry I was s-such a b-bitch this morning."

"Nah. You had a scare."

She leaned away from him to look into his eyes. "I'm sorry we won't have an extra day or two."

It hurt Fin's heart to hear the words, but talking her out of going home to her uncle would be not only impossible but pure selfish.

"Me too. But you know where you need to be."

No, he wouldn't be a selfish prick and try to talk her

into staying, but he wasn't a saint either. He knew full and well that this was his last chance to let her know how he felt and to let her know how much he wanted to see her again. And he wasn't going to let it pass him by.

"In Dublin," he said, reaching for her cheek to wipe away her tears, "my favorite bar is called Donoghue's. It's near St. Stephen's Green. Black-and-white front. Bit o' a dive inside. It's where the Dubliners got their start." Her eyes were luminous as she stared at him. "On Sundays, I play guitar there sometimes. If we get some fellas together, we might go on for two hours or more. It's the best place in Dublin." She scanned his face, nodding at him to let him know she was listening. "Now. Picture an old guy in the corner. Gray beard, white hair. He watches the door like it'll run away if he doesn't guard it, like he'll miss somethin' if he looks away."

"Do you know him?"

"I *am* him," said Fin. "In sixty years, that's me…still waitin' for you."

Her eyebrows knitted together in confusion. "What? What do you—?"

"I'll be there every Sunday at four, Tate, no matter what. No matter who gets married or who dies on a Sunday, I'll be there. I'll be watchin' the door for you to walk through it, darlin'. Nothin' will keep me away. I'll be waitin'."

"Fin," she sobbed, her tears falling fresh all over again.

"I didn't mean to get attached. I didn't mean to fall for you, *mo cailleach*. I didn't mean to, but I did. And all I want…" He gripped her cheeks harder, blinking his eyes against his own tears, as she reached up and covered his hands with her own. "*All I want*…is more time…with you."

She leaned forward, pressing her lips to his, their tears mingling as they shared the sorrow of bad timing and the rush of finding each other. Despite the odds, Fin somehow fit into the puzzle of her life like he was destined to be there all along.

"And now I'll drive you home," he whispered, leaning his forehead against hers one final time before helping her back into her seat and pulling back onto the highway.

chapter nine

One month later

"Finian!"

In his usual corner spot, he looked up to see a blonde woman walking toward him. For just a second, he thought it was Tate, and his heart—his *ridiculous* heart—swelled with hope.

But it wasn't Tate. It never was.

It was Cynthia, with pasty faced Jamie Gallagher nipping at her heels like a wee terrier. Fuck.

"Hello, Finian."

"'lo, Cindy," he greeted her with a wan smile.

"Anyone sittin' with you?" she asked, looking around the packed bar.

"It's mad here," added Jamie.

It's always mad on a Sunday, he thought, giving Jamie an unwelcome look.

"Eh…no," he said, wishing someone else would come and join him. Anyone. The bloody queen o' England would be more welcome than these two. "Though me mates could be by in a bit."

"How about we sit with you until they get here?" she suggested, taking a seat.

"Yeah. Grand," he said, though his tone stated it was anything but.

"So," said Jamie, in his pressed fucking golf shirt. *Twat.* "Cynthia says you went abroad for a while. How was that?"

"Yeah. Good. Thanks."

Cindy picked up her pint, wiggling her fingers against the glass as she took a wee drink, and it was impossible to ignore the ring she was wearing.

Oh, fer fuck's sake.

"New ring?" he asked.

"Engaged!" she crowed with a satisfied grin. "Jamie asked me."

"Didn't think the baby Jesus did."

"Blasphemy," whispered Jamie, looking horrified.

"You look like shite," said Cynthia sweetly.

Finian took a long drink of his beer, staring at her like he wished she'd get lost.

"We're gettin' married in August," she said, very pleased with herself.

"Knocked up?" asked Fin.

"*Gabh síos ort fhéin,*" growled Cynthia, which roughly translated to the suggestion that Finian go fuck himself.

"Cynthia!" gasped Jamie.

"Better me wankin' myself than puttin' up with the likes 'o you," he muttered.

"Well. I'll tell you one thing! *We're* not puttin' up with *this* a moment longer," said Jamie, rising from his seat. "Come along, Cynthia."

"Yeah. Good. Go fuck yerselves," said Fin, watching them go.

He finished his beer and slammed the glass down on

the wooden table.

Fucking Cynthia was getting married. Well, that was great. Bloody weapon. He wished her a hundred years of tepid sex with her pasty-faced grocer.

But on one count and one alone, Cynthia was probably right. He probably *did* look like shite.

It hadn't exactly been the best month of his life.

When he'd first gotten home, it'd been good to see his mam and dad and the lads. His old job was waiting for him, and his mates Colin and Tommy had offered him a spare room at their flat until he got set up again. In some ways, it was good to be home…but in others, it wasn't.

The first week, he'd still been on a high from meeting Tate and hopeful that she'd suddenly stroll into the bar one weekend, excited to see him. They'd connected over Facebook and Instagram and Skyped a few times too. But the distance was an unholy bitch, and he could feel her slipping away from him. He could feel all of that beautiful fucking potential fading day by day. And he hated it.

From what she said, her uncle was doing much better, but she was still nervous to leave him. Which had made Fin start wondering if she'd *ever* leave him. The more time that went by, the more he thought that she probably wouldn't. And the biggest problem with her reticence to visit was that Fin had already used up his immigration allowance for the year. He'd spent ninety days in the United States from October to December and another ninety days from January to March. Technically, he wasn't allowed back until next year.

So if Tate wouldn't come and see him? They were fucked.

Not that he had anything better to do than sit in this fucking corner every weekend. In fact, in a weird and likely masochistic twist of fate, he actually felt closest to her here. And deep in his heart, the hope that she would one day show up was the only thing that kept him sane.

He sighed, looking up to see if a waitress was passing by or if he'd have to give up his coveted seat to go get his own beer.

And that's when he saw her.

Platinum-blonde hair.

Blue eyes like the summer sky.

Dressed in jeans and a T-shirt, she stood about twelve feet away from him in the crowded bar.

Tate.

Tate.

Tate is here.

A million times, he'd imagined how it would feel to see her, but now that she was actually here? He froze for a moment just watching her, just processing the beautiful fucking reality that the woman he desperately wanted was finally, finally, finally…*here.*

His adrenaline skyrocketed, and he bolted up, heart racing, crossing to her in a moment and pushing two blokes out of the way to stand before her.

"Tate!"

"Fin!" she cried, throwing her arms around his neck.

He lifted her feet off the ground, yanking her against his chest and slamming his mouth against hers. Their teeth clacked together, but they were undeterred, kissing hard and fast in the dense crowd of a spring Sunday at Donoghue's. When he drew away, he was panting with surprise, his pulse zooming like a runaway train.

"Yer feckin' here."

"I'm fucking here."

"What're you drinkin'?"

"Beer," she said, grinning up at him as her feet touched back down on the floor.

"That's my table," he said, thumbing toward the corner.

"Just where you said."

"Like I promised."

"I'll sit."

"I'll get our drinks."

***

In the many dreams she'd had of their reunion, it had never included a packed-to-the-gills bar that smelled distinctly of wooden floorboards saturated with hundreds of years of spilled beer. And yet, as she slipped into the corner booth with its roughhewn wooden table, she realized that it was so perfectly Fin, it was perfect for her too.

He joined her a moment later, placing two pints of beer on the table and sliding in beside her, caressing her face with his eyes like he couldn't believe she was sitting next to him.

"You didn't tell me you were comin'."

She shrugged. "It was a last-minute decision."

"I'm so...Jaysus, I can't believe yer here. I'm so bloody glad to see you." Her hands were resting on the table, and he took the one closest to him and held it. "How's Pete?"

Her uncle had taken to calling her "warden" over the past month, griping that she was cramping his style by coming over every night to make him dinners that consisted of fish or chicken and vegetables.

Three days ago, when she'd stopped by with some

broiled cod and grilled zucchini, she'd been surprised to find Pete at the candlelit kitchen table, having dinner with a friend, Lucy Rodriguez. It had taken her a couple of minutes—and observing that her uncle was wearing a dress shirt—to realize that Pete wasn't *just* "having dinner." He was on a date, and by stopping by, she was interrupting. Awkwardly, she'd left the food on the kitchen counter, said good-bye, and left, but Pete had followed her.

"Tate Maureen, wait up."

Standing in the moonlight in his backyard, he'd pulled her gruffly into a bear hug. "You don't have to go."

"I think I do." She drew away and looked up at the face she loved so well. "At least you made chicken."

"Lucy made it," said Pete. "*And* the rice is brown."

"I approve," said Tate, kissing his cheek.

"Got you something, honey," he said, turning back to the house. "Wait there."

A moment later, he'd returned, offering her an envelope.

"What's this?"

"Your birthday present."

"You usually give me a gift card."

"Yeah, well. Things are different this year. I'm counting my blessings."

She'd opened the envelope to find a ticket to Dublin leaving in three days.

"Your vessel's still in dry dock for a month or so, and I figure…there's a guy over there waiting for you, right?"

With tears in her eyes, she'd thrown her arms around her uncle, squeezing him tightly. "I can't leave you."

"Honey, you are the best niece an old man could ask

for. But I got Lucy inside there waiting on me. And you gotta go find *your* Lucy. Well, that's not quite what I mean. But…you gotta go live your life, Tate Maureen." He'd kissed her cheek, the scruff of his beard scratching her skin. "Your momma would've been so proud of you."

How's Pete?

"He's good," she said, taking a sip of her beer and squeezing Fin's fingers. "Actually, *he* bought me the ticket to come over."

"He did?"

She nodded. "*And* he has a girlfriend."

"Salty dog!" exclaimed Finian, grinning at her. He bit his bottom lip, his smile fading just a touch. "How long are you stayin'?"

She took a deep breath. "Well…my yacht won't be ready for four more weeks."

Finian's mouth dropped open. "A month?"

"Too long?" she asked, grimacing slightly, hoping that he wanted her to stay just as much as she wanted to be with him.

"Not enough," he said, leaning forward to drop a kiss to her forehead, his voice warm with relief. "But it's good, Tate. A good start. I'll take it."

"Fin," she said, clutching his hand as she turned her face to his. "I live in Florida, and you live here. I wish I could, but I can't make you any promises. I'm seeing a therapist, but I'm still scared as hell."

"You're here," he said softly. "That's all that matters. We'll find our way, Tate. We'll figure it out together."

She bit her bottom lip, then let it go, looking into his eyes, scared to say the next words, but knowing he deserved to hear them.

"I don't know how good I'll be at loving someone, but I know this, Fin." She gulped. "I know I want to be loved."

Palming her cheeks with his hands, he drew her lips to his and kissed them tenderly.

"Then me darlin' girl, *mo cailleach*, my sweet Tate, you're in *exactly* the right place."

THE END

**What's happening with the Summerhaven trio?
Turn the page to read a letter from Katy!**

A LETTER FROM KATY

Dear reader,

Thank you so much for reading my Summerhaven series! I hope you've loved the stories of Rory, Tierney, Ian, and their cousin Finian. I certainly loved writing them.

Now I'm betting that some of you are wishing for some sort of epilogue here—something that wraps up Fin and Tate's story into a pretty bow and also manages to tell you that *all* of the Havens are doing well. I get that. I like that kind of closure too.

The thing is? I didn't plan to write an epilogue for this book, because it would be fake to give you the marriage of Fin and Tate when they're a long way from the altar. Are they crazy about each other? Yes. Are they going to end up together? Of course! But they still have a lot to figure out.

So instead of an epilogue, how about I give you a shorthand update on how everyone's doing, huh? Would that work? Yes? Good?

Okay. Here goes.

Brittany gave birth to a daughter in May. She and Rory named her Kendall, and her godparents are Tierney and Ian, which makes Jenny her adoring godsister. Their business—opening high-end camps for corporate retreats all over the world under the Manion brand—has taken off, and Rory is now a man of considerable means, though his greatest fortune is his girls. He and Britt still live in her Boston apartment, though they are building a five-bedroom "cottage" on land adjacent to Summerhaven. They plan to spend every summer up on the lake, which means another generation of Havens, starting with Jenny and Kendall, will grow up there together.

Tierney was married to Burr in June in a traditional Irish wedding. It lasted a full weekend, with Jenny and Bridey dressed up as the cutest flower girls ever seen, while Britt and Hallie served as matrons of honor. Tate came up from Florida for the weekend and did a reading from the book of Corinthians. Burr's sister, Suzanne, and her husband, Connor, are regular visitors at Summerhaven, and Burr has risen to the rank of sergeant at the local police department. Lately, Ian has noticed that Tierney always looks varying colors of green and carries saltines with her wherever she goes. But he figures she'll share her news when she's ready.

Speaking of Ian, like his brother, his greatest joy is also his girls: Hallie and Jenny...although that's going to change—in a good way!—soon! He found out this August that Hallie is pregnant with twin boys, which should even out the male-female ratio among the Haven cousins no matter what Tierney has! Hallie is due in February, and Jenny can't stop talking about being a big sister. Luckily, she's got her cousin, Kendall, for practice. As for Hallie's cottage? As a wedding gift, Brittany paid for it to be renovated on the sly, and it's on its way to becoming a storybook four-bedroom cottage, perfect for a growing family.

As for our newest couple, Finian and Tate...after they spent most of April together in Ireland, Tate had to return to Florida. But she went back to Ireland for two weeks in June, two weeks in July, and another two weeks in August. When she returned to Florida in August, Uncle Pete announced that he had proposed to Miss Lucy. After their marriage, they planned to move closer to Lucy's family in Puerto Rico, where they'd start a small charter business together.

This left Tate feeling a little left behind until Uncle Pete explained that he'd hired an immigration attorney to do some research for his niece. He'd learned that she needed $5 million in the bank to make an annual income of $50,000, the minimum required for an American to "retire" in the Emerald Isle and live there indefinitely. With his gentle urging, Tate sold her boat for $8.5 million, banked the profit, and surprised an overjoyed Fin when she announced that she was moving to Dublin. Last I heard, Tate was investing in a brand-new garage owned by a top-notch young mechanic who had a fondness for American girls and DeLoreans. And if my information is correct, they just put a bid on a two-bedroom harbor-view house in Howth, where Tate moors her modest, fifteen-foot yacht. Sounds like they're pretty happy.

Yes, friends, I'm delighted to report that my Havens are doing A-OK.

And that—in the business of romance writing—is what we call a very happy ending.

Love,
Katy
xoxoxo

THE ROUSSEAUS
(Blueberry Lane Books #12–14)

Jonquils for Jax
Marry Me Mad
J.C. and the Bijoux Jolis

THE STORY SISTERS
(Blueberry Lane Books #15–17)

The Bohemian and the Businessman
The Director and Don Juan
Countdown to Midnight

_a   m o d e r n   f a i r y t a l e_
(A collection)

The Vixen and the Vet
Never Let You Go
Ginger's Heart
Dark Sexy Knight
Don't Speak
Shear Heaven

Fragments of Ash
Coming 2018

Swan Song
Coming 2018

STAND-ALONE BOOKS:

After We Break
(a stand-alone second-chance romance)

Frosted
(a romance novella for mature readers)

Unloved, a love story
(a stand-alone suspenseful romance)

ABOUT THE AUTHOR

New York Times **and** *USA Today* **best-selling author Katy Regnery** started her writing career by enrolling in a short story class in January 2012. One year later, she signed her first contract, and Katy's first novel was published in September 2013.

Forty books later, Katy claims authorship of the multititled *New York Times* and *USA Today* best-selling Blueberry Lane Series, which follows the English, Winslow, Rousseau, Story, and Ambler families of Philadelphia; the six-book, bestselling ~a modern fairytale~ series; and several other stand-alone novels and novellas, including the critically acclaimed, 2018 RITA® nominated, *USA Today* bestselling contemporary romance *Unloved, a love story.*

Katy's first modern fairytale romance, *The Vixen and the Vet*, was nominated for a RITA® in 2015 and won the 2015 Kindle Book Award for romance. Katy's *The English Brothers Boxed Set*, Books #1–4, hit the *USA Today* bestseller list in 2015, and her Christmas story, *Marrying Mr. English*, appeared on the list a week later. In May 2016, Katy's Blueberry Lane collection, *The Winslow Brothers Boxed Set*, Books #1–4, became a *New York Times* e-book bestseller.

Katy's books are available in English, French, German, Italian, Portuguese, and Turkish.

Katy lives in the relative wilds of northern Fairfield

County, Connecticut, where her writing room looks out at the woods, and her husband, two young children, two dogs, and one Blue Tonkinese kitten create just enough cheerful chaos to remind her that the very best love stories begin at home.

Sign up for Katy's newsletter today:
www.katyregnery.com!

CPSIA information can be obtained
at www.ICGtesting.com
Printed in the USA
LVHW081210170219
607706LV00030B/450/P

9 781944 810351